A KIND OF SECRET WEAPON

A
KIND OF
SECRET
WEAPON

ELLIOTT ARNOLD

CHARLES SCRIBNER'S SONS

NEW YORK

PRINTED IN THE UNITED STATES OF AMERICA
SBN 684-81963-5
LIBRARY OF CONGRESS CATALOG CARD NUMBER 69-12598

FOR

WOODY, CHRIS, JEFF AND TIMOTHY

AND FOR

SUSIE

THE YOUNGEST CHILD OF THEM ALL

1

IT STARTED FOR PETER ON A DAY IN DECEMBER WHEN HE RE-turned home from school and went down to the basement to get his ice-skates.

He found his mother and father hunched over a mimeograph machine. His father was cranking the machine. His mother was carefully collecting the sheets of paper that leaped out.

Because of the noise of the machine neither parent heard Peter come down the stairs. His father continued to crank, and his mother continued to collect the papers and stack them in a neat pile.

That was the way Peter always remembered it, the cellar warm from the furnace, the little windows that were level with the ground outside covered with blackout curtains, the sound of the machine, even and orderly and rhythmic as the ticking of the grandfather clock upstairs, his mother and father intent on what they were doing, so concentrated they seemed in some private place of their own. At that moment they appeared to Peter to be strangers.

Peter stood there, feeling an intruder in his own home in the presence of his mother and his father, and he was almost at the point of backing quietly up the stairs when his mother brushed her hair away from her eyes and happened to glance up and see him. From the sudden frown on her face he knew he was an intruder.

7

His mother said, "Lars." She said it in a low voice. When Peter's father did not look up, she said it again, in the same still voice, "Lars."

This time Lars Andersen looked up, first at his wife, and then at what she was staring. He stopped cranking the machine and the basement was instantly silent. Lars Andersen and his wife looked at their son.

"What's the matter?" Peter asked. When they did not reply, he asked, "What are you doing?"

"Go upstairs, Peter," Lise said. Peter had never known that sound in her voice.

"But what are you doing?"

"Nothing you need to know about. What are you doing down here?" It was still the voice of a stranger.

"I wanted to get my ice-skates." He felt frightened, and he had never felt frightened with his parents before. "The pond is frozen solid." He walked toward them as though that somehow might lessen the fear. He looked at the mimeograph machine and at the neat pile of papers. "What are you doing?"

"Nothing that concerns you," Lise said angrily. "Get your skates and go to the pond and just forget anything you've seen here." She looked at the boy's bewildered face and rushed to him and put her arms around him. "Please, Peter, don't ask any questions, and please forget all about this and don't say anything about it to any of your friends. Promise me."

"I promise," Peter said automatically. He looked again at the machine and then at his father.

"It's important," Lise said rapidly. "You must not talk about this."

8

"Has it got something to do with the war?" the boy asked. "Has it got something to do with the Germans?"

Lise shook her head. "Peter, you mustn't ask any questions, and you must forget about this."

"No," Lars Andersen said. It was the first word he had spoken.

"Get your skates," Lise said. She looked around. "There, I see them over there. Yes, there they are. Now get them and join your friends."

"No," Lars said again.

She turned fiercely on her husband. "Lars, he's only a child."

Lars Andersen straightened slowly. He was a tall, thin man with long, thin fingers and his bones were very close to his skin, and there was very little flesh on them; no matter how much he ate, even in the old days when food in Denmark was something to talk about, not even then was he ever able to put on weight.

That was how Peter always remembered it: first the two of them bent over the machine; and then now, his tall, skinny father whose coat sleeves were always too short; and the shock of hair that looked as though it had been blown into a heap by a winter wind; the long face and the wide mouth that always had a kind of smile on it as though Lars Andersen lived with a private joke. And his mother, small and dark, with her little oval face that also had a smile that belonged there, a sudden, burst of a smile that was like a light turned on.

But there was no trace of that smile now. There was pleading in her face, and the face was heavy with strain and fear and worry. And defeat.

"Peter," Lise said again, and now her voice was lost.

The boy walked past his mother and he saw there were tiny, bright dots of tears in her eyes and later he realized something was happening, something important, something he would never forget, something that was changing him so he would never again be the boy who had walked down the cellar stairs to find his ice-skates.

Lars Andersen picked up one of the sheets of paper from the tidy pile Lise had made. He held it toward his son. Peter took it and looked at it. The words A LIBERATED DENMARK were printed in large letters across the top of the page, and the rest of the page was divided into columns filled with type. Lise's eyes were dull as she watched.

"Do you know what that is, Peter?" Lars asked.

"It looks like a little newspaper."

"Exactly. But it is a special kind of little newspaper. Can you imagine what kind it is?"

"It has to do with the Germans. It has to do with the war."

Lars Andersen nodded slowly. "It has very much to do with both of those, the Germans and the war. That, son, is an underground paper. That's why we print it in the basement." Lars Andersen chuckled at his own joke. "Come on, Lise," he said, looking at his wife. "My goodness, your face is so long you'll stumble on it. It's time Peter knew."

Peter felt a prickle of excitement. "Underground paper," he repeated. "Then it's illegal, if the Germans . . ."

Lars grinned. "If the Germans . . . But the Germans won't. The Germans are not all that clever. They say they are and they think they are and they say it so often people even begin to believe they are, but they're really not. Oh, they have some clever men among them, but even they are a little stupid because they think they're twice as clever as they are."

Peter looked again at the sheet of paper. There was a story about a bridge that was blown up so a German troop train bound for Norway was delayed for three days. There was a story about how the last of the Danish Jews had been taken safely to Sweden. There was a story about the disappearance and presumable death of three young Danish saboteurs who were arrested by the Gestapo.

Peter looked up. "I never knew things like this were happening."

"Exactly!" Lars said heartily. "And you have just stated the precise reason for the existence of this small newspaper. It is to print things that the Germans will not allow us to print in my big newspaper or in any other newspaper in Denmark. It's to put down these things so that other Danes will know we are doing a few small things against the enemy."

Peter's forehead puckered, and he looked again at the small sheet of paper. He read over again about the last of the Jews having been taken to Sweden. He had wondered about that. There were three or four Jewish boys and girls in his class, and they had quite suddenly vanished one day. It was only after they were gone and he asked another boy what had happened to them and the boy didn't know either and they had both questioned the teacher that they found out that their missing schoolmates were Jews. He had never known that before. He was not even quite sure what a Jew was, but he did know that the Germans for some reason hated them and that for almost four years the Germans had done nothing about it; then they decided to do something about it, but the Danes did something first. What the Danes did, Peter had found out, was get their fellow citizens out of the country so that in the end the Germans were able to lay their hands on only slightly more than four hundred of the eight thousand Danish Jews.

Peter had heard things about that and now he was seeing something to do with it in print, along with other things, in a secret, home-made paper his mother and father got out.

"Where do you find out about these things?" he asked his father.

"Lars," Lise said in a voice as dull as her eyes. "The boy has heard quite enough."

"He has not," Lars Andersen said. "And don't call him 'the boy.' His name is Peter, and it's a fine name, and he should be addressed by it." Then he looked doubtfully at Peter. "Perhaps your mother is right," he said.

"No," Peter said. "Father, please."

Lars Andersen looked at his son for a long time. Then he said, "Let me put it to you, Peter. How would you suppose we gathered this information?"

Peter loved the way his father used words. They sometimes were a little grander words than most people generally used. But then his father was a writer on one of the biggest newspapers in Copenhagen.

He thought for a moment or two and then shook his head. "I don't know, Father."

Lars Andersen leaned forward. "Think, Peter. Put that big blob of gray matter to work. Let me give you a hint. What kind of work do I do? Officially, I mean."

"You're a journalist."

"Exactly. Now, we know that the Germans won't let us print anything they consider harmful to their side. We know that, don't we?"

"Yes, Father."

"Good. Well, that means they must censor the newspapers. Now, if they censor the ordinary papers—do you know what 'censor' means, Peter?"

"Of course. Keep things out."

"Well, that's half of it. It also means putting things in, false things. But if they are able to keep things out, what does that mean?"

Peter bit his lip. Then he looked up. "That means you hear things you aren't allowed to print."

Lars broke into a wide grin. "High marks for that." He turned to his wife who had not stopped staring at her son. "A child? My goodness, you forget he soon will be twelve. In some parts of the world boys who have reached that exalted age are given rifles to defend their country."

"And the stories the Germans censor, the things they won't let you put in the Copenhagen newspaper, you put them in this little paper," Peter said excitedly.

"Peter, in the last few minutes you have raised my opinion of you considerably," Lars Andersen said. "I always had the feeling that perhaps you inherited too much from your mother, but you have now persuaded me that some small quantity of your father's intelligence has also managed to seep through." He nodded approvingly. "It couldn't have worked out better. Your mother's beauty and your father's brains. I think we did very well, Lise."

She looked away from Peter and toward her husband and now Peter saw the little smile at the edges of her mouth, and then she shook her head helplessly.

"Now," Lars Andersen said. "Now that Peter knows our terrible secret we must make him pay for that knowledge and put him to work."

The smile on Lise's face vanished. "No," she said.

"Strong hands," Lars said. "Willing fingers."

"I don't want him involved in this," Lise said.

"He is involved in this," Lars said very gently. "He is involved because he knows, and he is quite properly involved. This is his country just as it is your country and my country, and he is not quite the infant you make him out to be. And when all of this stupidity is ended and the Germans go home to dirty their own land, he should have a memory of some kind, a memory he will be proud of, a memory of having in some way, no matter how small, participated in the Resistance." He turned to Peter. "Do you understand what I am saying, son?"

"Yes," Peter said.

"Do you agree with what I have said?"

"Yes, Father."

"Would you like to help with our little paper?"

"Oh, yes!"

"Oh, yes," Lise repeated in a small voice.

"You know there is a certain amount of danger in all this?"

"That's exciting."

"Then you agree."

Peter nodded vehemently.

Lars Andersen held out his hand in an oddly solemn manner. Peter looked at the outstretched hand, and then took it.

"Done," Lars Andersen said. "Lise, our staff has just been increased."

14

Lise breathed out heavily. "I suppose it was inevitable."

"Inevitable," Lars agreed. "Inevitable and fortunate. You understand, Peter, that your mother was quite right about one thing. Nothing must be said about this. Not a word, not a single word—to no one."

"Of course not," Peter said indignantly. "Do you think I'm a baby?"

"No," Lise said. "No one thinks that. No one thinks that any more."

Lars clapped his hands and rubbed them. "All right, back to work. We've still a few hundred of these to run off. Peter, would you like to report for work immediately, or would you still prefer to go off ice-skating?"

"You know what I'd rather do," Peter said.

Lars looked sad and shrugged his shoulders. "All right, son, go ahead, have a good time and don't fall on the ice."

"Father!"

Lise pointed. "There is string. Bundles of about two hundred and fifty sheets. No more. They mustn't look too bulky, and we have to be able to get rid of them in case of trouble."

2

THE ANDERSENS LIVED IN THE LITTLE TOWN OF SNEKKER-sten, which was located on the west coast of Sealand on the Sound just below Elsinore. It was a lovely place, especially now in the winter with the early snow still on the ground and the trees dangling slender icicles that sparkled in the sunlight. It was a very pretty little place and ordinarily a good place for a boy to live and grow up. It soon would be even prettier with Christmas and all the excitement and beauty that went with the holiday season.

But these were not ordinary times. This was the winter of 1943; the Nazis had occupied Denmark for more than three-and-a-half years, and a boy like Peter could hardly remember a time when the Germans were not there.

It was true that for a long time after they swept into the small country of Denmark in May of 1940 the Germans had behaved carefully. Their leader, Adolf Hitler, had wanted to show the world that the Danes, given the chance, would be happy to be a part of his Europe, and he gave the Danes that chance.

For a long while, until quite recently, life had been reasonably peaceful in the tiny Scandinavian kingdom. Very few persons wanted the Germans on their necks, but there was nothing they could do about it, and being practical people they had put up with it as best they could. And the Germans had done as little as possible to offend them, even to the point of leaving the Jews alone, making Denmark the only German-occupied country in which Jews were not molested.

But late in September of 1943, Hitler issued orders to round up all the Danish Jews. He sent freighters to collect them and take them to concentration camps for extermination. At this, the Danes took a stand. They refused to permit it. They themselves gathered their fellow citizens and in a miracle of organization got them all over to Sweden. This act of defiance infuriated the Germans, and

16

the Danes, flushed with their unexpected success, decided to go on to bigger things.

The Danish Resistance, which before the attempted action against the Danish Jews had consisted of splinter groups of uncoordinated saboteurs, now was a guerilla force of skill and strength and experience; they had taken the measure of the Germans and had defeated them. And now the sabotage was becoming more and more serious, and these were the things Lars Andersen and scores of other underground publishers were reporting with such pleasure not only to the people of Denmark but to the world as well.

These thoughts were very much in Peter's mind the next day as he trudged off to school. He was tingling with excitement, of course, knowing what was going on in his house. He had hardly slept, and he was proud his parents were doing what they were and that they now were allowing him to be part of the adventure.

He was not altogether surprised that his father was doing this because his father was a newspaperman and before the war had traveled a great deal for his paper. He was in Peter's eyes a very special person, beyond the fact that he was his father. No, now that he thought about it, it seemed perfectly natural that his father would be involved in this mysterious work. What surprised him more than anything else was that his mother was a part of the scheme as well. His mother was, well, quiet. Not unhappy quiet, no. His mother was happy, and the home was a happy home, but somehow he never would have imagined his mother would be doing anything so dangerous. And they had made it clear to him it was dangerous.

Peter was stirred as he walked down the lane from his house and then turned into the larger road that led to the main coast highway. Overnight, his parents had become quite different, and his house had become a different house; and now he was in possession of the secret too, and he was part of it.

He reached the coast road and he looked at the Sound under the leaden winter sky and across the Sound to Sweden, where he had been taken often before the war. He didn't remember much about Sweden, but now with the new things that were happening to him, he paused and looked over the narrow body of water that separated the two countries, and he wondered how things were over there in that land, so close but now so different.

The wind blew in from the water and nibbled on his ears. In the summers, in the old days, and he could remember this, the little fishing port was always filled with boats —fishing boats, pleasure boats, little skiffs. There was always excitement in the summer and many visitors from foreign countries on their way up to Elsinore to see Kronborg, Hamlet's castle.

Now, because of German orders, all the pleasure boats had to be kept on dry land, dragged back a certain, specified distance from the water. The fishing boats were allowed to go about their business, of course, because the Danes depended so much on their catch for food, and the Germans were taking a great deal of that catch themselves to feed Germans, those in Germany and those stationed in Denmark. Those fishing boats had proved to be the salvation of the Jews in their forced exodus from their homeland.

18

As Peter walked toward school, his mind filled with many things, none of them to do with school, he was joined by his friend, Kai Madsen. The two boys bent their heads against the wind.

"What happened to you yesterday?" Kai asked, shouting, because of the wind.

"Yesterday?" Peter repeated, startled. What had Kai found out?

"The skating was wonderful."

"The skating." Peter lowered his head still farther to hide the relief on his face. He had forgotten all about the frozen pond and the skating and the fact that he had promised Kai he would join him.

"Are you all right?" Kai asked.

"All right?"

"You seem funny."

"Well, I wasn't feeling too well yesterday. That's why I didn't go skating. My mother thought I might be catching a cold."

"Are you?"

"No, I feel fine today. Did you have fun at the pond?"

Kai told him enthusiastically how much fun it had been and how now it looked as though it might snow again, and it might be a time before the pond would be clear again. He chattered on until they reached the school, and all the time Peter was chuckling to himself thinking how surprised Kai would be if he told him what had really happened when he returned home from school the day before.

As the two boys were entering the school Peter saw the huge, black German car that belonged to the chief of the

Gestapo in Elsinore. And inside the car was the man himself, Major Heinz Gruber, his big, red face grim, his eyes staring straight ahead, past his driver and the other Gestapoman seated in the front of the car.

There was a funny story about Gruber. Whenever he set out to arrest someone—and this was happening more and more these days—he would be seen passing in the black car and Danes would get on the telephone immediately and warn whoever they thought he was looking for. Anyone who had any reason to believe he might be picked up by the Gestapo would go into hiding immediately. Major Gruber rarely found his quarry at home.

This angered the Nazi officer, naturally, and he thought about it and worked out what he considered a clever ruse. Instead of using his official automobile, which was recognized immediately, he began to use ordinary taxicabs when he went out to arrest Danes.

Of course he was much less conspicuous riding in a taxi than he was in his car, but he was equally unsuccessful. What he hadn't realized was that when he ordered a cab from the company in Elsinore and gave his destination, the manager knew exactly where he was going and instead of there having to be many telephone calls made to alert possible victims, it was necessary only to call the person Major Gruber was going to.

It was after four or five fruitless sallies that Major Gruber realized something was wrong, and he returned to his own vehicle. If he did not find the man he was seeking, at least there would not be a Danish cab driver, waiting with expressionless face, to drive him back to his office.

Major Gruber, because of the game that was constantly played with him, was something of a private joke in that part of Denmark; someone who contributed to the Danish sense of humor, which did not have much to feed on these days.

But seeing the car pass with the man inside, Peter did not at that moment think he was funny at all. For now he, Peter Andersen, was directly involved with Major Heinz Gruber and the whole, vast machinery of the Nazi Gestapo.

It was a thought that made Peter draw in his breath sharply. For a moment he wished he had not come upon his parents' illegal activities. For a moment he wished he had nothing on his mind but his school work and Christmas and when the pond could be skated on again. For that moment he was frightened, very frightened. And he wondered whether he was man enough to know what he now knew.

He would have to be man enough, he thought, because he was not only involved with Major Gruber; he also was involved with his mother and father.

As he walked down the corridor toward his classroom, nodding to other boys and girls, he could not immediately find any answer to his fears. He knew he must try to conquer them and regain some of the pride and excitement he had felt since he was made part of the secret.

But while he was not very old, he was old enough to know he could not find the answer until the time of testing came. It would only be then that he would find out whether he was brave or cowardly, manly or childish, worthy or unworthy.

As the tall, slender, fair-haired boy entered his classroom, it seemed a foreign place.

21

3

FOR SEVERAL DAYS THERE WAS NOTHING MORE SAID IN THE Andersen house about the unlawful little newspaper. It was as though Lars and Lise had had second thoughts about letting Peter help. Peter did not know whether to feel relieved or let down.

Then one afternoon as he was returning from school, he caught up with his mother in the lane leading to their house. Lise was walking, pushing her bicycle up a slight incline. The basket between the handlebars was piled high with fruits and vegetables.

As Peter ran up to her she paused, and he saw she was breathing a little heavily and that despite the freezing weather there were little beads of perspiration on her upper lip.

Lisa smiled at him, catching her breath, and then before she realized what he was doing, he hung his briefcase on one of the handlebars and took the bicycle from her.

"What's the matter, Mother, are you getting weak?" Peter asked. He gave the cycle a shove, and then he stopped. "Gosh, what have you got in there, a load of bricks?"

"Give it back to me," Lise said sharply.

But by then Peter had pushed the net shopping bags aside and was staring at a large package tied with heavy cord.

"Gosh, what's in that? It must weigh a ton."

Lise was silent for a moment. Then she said, "Paper."

22

"Paper? What kind of paper?" Then Peter looked up at her, knowing.

"Your father will be very happy," Lise said quietly. "That's one of our big problems, paper."

She took hold of one of the handlebars and he took the other and they walked slowly toward the house, wheeling the bicycle between them.

"Such simple things," Lise said. "Paper. Ink for the stencils. The stencils themselves. Money to pay for them. They're harder to get than the news itself."

"Where do you get them?"

"The money is simplest. We just ask friends. Little contributions."

"And all the rest?"

"Anywhere and everywhere. Paper mills. Stationery stores. Sometimes your father can get paper from his newspaper in Copenhagen, but they have to be very careful. The Germans are everywhere."

"Where did you get this batch?"

"Perhaps you'd better not know. You're burdened enough as it is."

"I'd never say anything. I promised."

"I know. But it's safer if you don't know."

They continued on toward the house. Peter thought of his mother, who was smaller than he was, and of Major Heinz Gruber, so huge, in his huge car, and he looked at her almost shyly. He thought of her going to the market and buying the fruit and vegetables and then going to wherever it was she went for the paper and covering the paper with the things from the market and then pushing the bicycle through the town. And he thought of what would happen to her if Major Gruber or any of the other

23

Germans stopped her and asked to have a look.

It was funny. You thought of your parents in different kinds of ways. You loved them, but sometimes you wished they weren't so strict, that they didn't tell you you couldn't do this or you had to do that. You knew they were always there when you needed them, if you were sick or hurt yourself, and they were proud of you when you got good marks in school and were disappointed when you didn't. But the thing was you thought of them only in connection with yourself, as though that was what made their life, the way it had to do with you.

And now he was finding it all was different. Here was his mother, who cooked meals and made beds and had cookies and milk waiting when he got back from school, who mended clothes and washed dishes—and she was also doing something that had nothing to do with their family life.

His mother was challenging the Germans.

It was a staggering thought. It was more than just stacking piles of paper in the basement. It was something out of an adventure story, and his mother never had been anyone he thought belonged in an adventure story.

His mother, who was frightened about so many things —woman kind of fright: snakes, thunder, the great ocean waves—who turned her head away when Peter or his father put a worm on a fishing hook, who couldn't bear to see the fish flopping around before they died—his mother was challenging the Germans.

He looked at her again. She looked no different. She was the same person. But she was also someone else entirely.

They reached the house and leaned the bicycle

against the front steps. Peter found he too was slightly out of breath. He wondered where his mother had found the strength to get as far as she had all by herself.

They wheeled the bicycle to the back of the house. Lise looked around to make certain they were alone, and then they removed the fruit and vegetables and lifted out the bundle. Peter slung it over his shoulder and carried it inside the house and down the steps to the cellar.

He set it down next to the mimeograph machine, now pushed into a corner and covered with an old tarpaulin.

When he went back upstairs into the kitchen, his mother was taking the food out of the net bags.

"It looks like everybody in the house has something to eat," he said.

His mother raised her eyes to him for a moment and then turned her head and took the last of the food out of the bags.

4

THE EXCITEMENT WAS NOT YET OVER FOR THAT DAY.

Lars Andersen returned about five o'clock. He took off his gloves and slapped his hands against the cold. He took a folded copy of his Copenhagen newspaper out of his coat pocket. He pointed to one of the articles.

"My literary style is definitely improving," he said.

Peter looked at the paper. There was a story on the front page with his father's name over it.

"I'll have to read it so I'll know what I wrote," Lars said with his funny smile.

"What do you mean, Father?" Peter asked. "I don't understand."

"Of course not. How could you?" Lars took off his overcoat. "You see, son, I never wrote that story."

"But it has your name on it."

"Many of my stories are being written for me these days. So the Germans won't get suspicious." When he saw Peter did not yet understand, he went on. "I don't have all the time to do my regular job."

"Because of the little paper."

"Because of the little paper. The other men at the paper take turns writing stories for me. The Nazis aren't altogether stupid. They read and they check. And this keeps them from asking questions."

He sat down and stretched his legs and then his eyes began to sparkle.

"There was a little unexpected noise in Jutland this afternoon," he said casually. "Another troop train on its way to Norway. It will be slightly delayed." He sat there for a moment. Then he looked at his watch and stood up.

"Lars," Lise said warningly.

"No secrets," Lars said. "No more secrets in this house."

He went to a cabinet and opened the doors. As Peter watched curiously, he removed several books, two bottles of aquavit, and an old-fashioned music box. He reached into the cabinet again and Peter, craning his neck, saw there was a small door in the back of the cabinet. His father opened the door, revealing a small enclosure, like a tiny wall safe. He reached into the enclosure and took out a small battery-operated short-wave radio.

"How do you like that, young man?" Lars asked holding out the radio.

"Gosh," Peter said.

"A present," Lars said. "A present from the RAF."

He nodded to Lise. She went to the front door and locked it.

"Draw the curtains, Peter," Lars said. He turned a switch on the radio.

A few moments later there was a crackling sound. Lars looked at his watch again. Then a voice with a British accent spoke quietly from the radio.

"This is the BBC London calling," the voice said.

The newscaster gave a résumé of the war news. Then Peter was amazed to hear the voice say, "We have just received information from German Occupied Denmark that a German military train on its way to Norway was derailed by explosives in Jutland. Initial information indicates the locomotive was seriously damaged, possibly destroyed. There were at least eight Germans killed and many others injured. This action by the Danish Resistance occurred less than four hours ago . . . A report has just arrived from Norway . . ."

Lars switched off the radio, put it back in the enclosure, closed the door, replaced the music box, the books and one of the bottles of aquavit.

"I think," he said, "this calls for a small celebration."

"Less than four hours ago," Peter said wonderingly. "How could they find out so quickly?"

"Your father," Lars said. "He's rather marvelous." He poured a drink. He peered at Lise. "Don't you think so?"

27

After dinner that night, before Peter started on his homework, he asked his father again. "How did they hear about it so quickly in London?"

"We have lots of ways," Lars said. "There are German planes, civilian planes, flying from here to Sweden. There are boats crossing all the time. There is the ferry at Elsinore. Never mind which method we used today. Whichever it was, it did the job effectively." He paused for a moment. "You know, son, this little extraneous activity your father is engaged in—do you know what 'extraneous' means?"

"Yes, sir."

"Well, it's going to make a better newspaperman out of me. A more accurate newspaperman, I should say." He chuckled. "Maybe that won't be so good. You see, we have to be very careful to get our facts exactly right. We should do that all the time on the regular newspaper, of course, but sometimes we get a little careless, or perhaps we want to make the story better than it is, and we bend the truth a little. But we can't fool around with the news in our little paper. Because the people here usually find out one way or another what happens near them. And then they read about it in the little paper. And it has to be exactly true, in every detail. Because if they find any mistakes in the stories they know about, they won't believe the other stories, the stories they don't know about. They must have complete faith in everything they read in our little paper, and in all the other little illegal papers that are being turned out all over Denmark. This is not the happiest time in our history, Peter, and they must believe that everything they read is precisely what happened. And not something just dreamed up to make them feel better."

Peter nodded. "Did you really get that little radio from the RAF?"

"Yes."

"How?"

"Air drops."

"What would happen if the Germans found out about the drops?"

"Oh, they know about them. They just can't do very much to stop them." He leaned toward his son. "You see, Peter, almost everybody in our little country despises the Nazis. When an RAF plane drops things, everybody co-operates and gathers them up and hides them. There just aren't enough Germans in Denmark to search every hiding place every day." He sat back and looked searchingly at his son. "I want you to know about these things and to think carefully about them because boys your age will be grown men soon and by then, with the help of God, the war will be over, and the Germans will be defeated. They will go back where they came from, and I want you then to be proud of Denmark. We may not be doing what the Norwegians are doing, but we don't have a big country full of mountains to hide in and fight from. But we are doing what we are able to do. And that's the important thing."

5

PETER COULD NOT FORGET IT. WHAT HIS FATHER HAD SAID to him filled his mind as he sat in his room and tried to concentrate on his homework.

He was still thinking about it when he finished and had bread and jam and a glass of milk. He thought about it after he climbed into bed.

It was some time later. He did not know whether he had slept and then wakened or whether he had not slept at all, but sometime during the night he knew he was awake, and he was hearing voices. Staring at the dark ceiling, he listened to the voices—the sound of voices, really, because he could not make out what was being said—and he found himself crawling out from under the blankets into the cold room. The voices came from below, from under the window of his bedroom and he tiptoed to the window, which was opened a little, and listened. He still could not make out words, but he recognized two of the voices. One was his father's, the other that of the pastor of their church, Palle Holm.

He knelt on the cold floor and looked down. It was not a bright night, but he could make out the figures of men. He recognized Pastor Holm, a large, powerfully-built man. He could make out the figure of his father. There was a third man, and it seemed to Peter that he was leaning against the priest and that Holm had his arm around him, supporting him.

His father was standing just outside the door, saying something in a whisper, and then he heard the voice of his mother, but he could not hear what she said either. Then he heard his father say clearly, "Of course, there's no question about it, no question at all."

Then there was movement down below, and all the figures entered the house. The front door was shut and the night was quiet. Peter found himself shivering, and he did not know whether it was because of the cold or because of something else entirely.

He hurried back into bed and pulled the covers up to his chin. He shook for a little while, and then he fell asleep. He was wakened by his father, telling him it was time to get up for school.

He started to tell Lars what he had seen and heard during the night, but he did not. As he was brushing his teeth, he wondered why he had kept silent. And oddly he came to understand that it was not because there were things going on from which he was still excluded but because he was part of the great secret, and by not telling and not asking he was playing his own part in the game.

But by the time he finished breakfast he had begun to wonder whether it had actually happened or whether it was something he had dreamed. His father was always talking about his imagination. With all the things he was finding out, it wouldn't be unusual to be having dreams like that.

But he was sure he could remember the voices and the man leaning against Pastor Holm. But his mother and father were acting perfectly normally; his father making his usual solemn, owlish jokes, his mother bustling about with the food.

And of course there was no sign of anybody in the house. Nobody could be in the house. It wasn't that large. There was no place anyone could be hidden.

He didn't know why he thought of the word "hidden." Even if what happened last night really happened and was not just part of a dream there was no reason to think anyone would have to be hidden. And yet there was the memory of the man leaning against Pastor Holm and the priest supporting him with his arm around his back.

As though there were something wrong with the man. As though he were hurt. Or wounded.

No place anyone could be hidden. Except the cellar. There were other things hidden in the cellar.

"Where are you?" he heard his father ask.

"Excuse me," Peter said.

"I've asked you something twice and you haven't answered," Lars said. "Where are you?" He snapped his fingers. "Love?"

"What?" Peter asked.

"Are you in love?"

"Father . . ."

"That must be it. Only some pretty young face could put that faraway look in your eyes. Who is she? Aska? Maren? The little Koch girl?"

"Let him eat his breakfast," Lise said. "You'll make him late for school."

"What an age," Lars said. "Going on twelve. All the facts of life emerging." He leaned toward Peter confidentially. "You know something, son, when I was your age . . ."

"Lars!"

Lars leaned back and sighed. "Yes, Lise, you're probably right. No use recalling those wonderful days, no use at all." Then he broke into a laugh. "Do you know something, Peter? I was a track star."

"I know that," Peter said.

"Yes, you know that because of the medals and the trophies. But what you don't know is that your mother was my greatest fan. She worshipped me."

"I did, did I?" Lise asked.

"Worshipped," Lars said. "It's the only word. She

used to come to all the track meets and stare at me with moon eyes. And you know something? It made me self-conscious, all that adoration flowing all over me. Why, it became so noticeable there was talk about barring little Lise Knudsen from the contests."

"Untrue," Lise said. "Absolutely untrue."

But Peter could see the twinkle in her eyes.

"They had a meeting," Lars went on. "The head coach and the assistant coach and even the principal of the school, to decide whether Lise Knudsen should be forbidden to attend the track meets because of her distracting effect on the star runner."

"And you pushed your way into that meeting without being invited and said if they did any such thing you would resign from the team," Lise said.

"Then it was true," Peter said.

"Yes, it was true," Lise said. "He was such a beanpole. So skinny. Skinnier than he is even now. I remember those big knobs of knees and those long, skinny legs, pumping up and down, up and down. He was like a crane running on the track, like a crane or a stork."

"But always the first across the line," Lars said.

"Almost always," Lise corrected.

"Almost always."

Lise giggled. "He must have looked so funny, defying the coaches and the principal. I've always tried to imagine that scene."

"Not funny at all," Lars said. "Dignified. Firm. Polite with my elders, but firm."

"That was when I knew that the great track star loved me," Lise said. "It's true. I thought he was marvelous but that was the first I realized he felt that way about me."

"Nonsense," Lars said. "It was simply a matter of principle. Barring people from athletic contests. Undemocratic! Un-Danish! Let them get away with that and no knowing what they'd try next. The thin edge of the wedge."

"Besides you liked to show off," Lise said. "You wanted your greatest admirer there to see how wonderful you were."

"Nonsense again. Everybody thought I was wonderful. What difference did one more or less make?" He sipped his coffee and looked at it disgustedly. "My goodness, what a horrible thing to have to drink in the morning. I think that as soon as this war is over and things return to normal, I'm going to drink a whole gallon of real coffee. A whole gallon."

"What if the Germans win?" Peter asked.

His father put down the cup. "I know you are joking, Peter," he said. "But you must not ever say that again, even in a joke. You must not even think it. Even the thought of such a thing would tend to corrode your soul. Do you know what 'corrode' means?"

"I think so."

"It's the greatest weapon the Germans have," Lars said soberly. "Greater than their guns and their planes and their tanks and their soldiers. Their propaganda. They've won many times because they convinced their opponents it was useless to fight against them. The ones who refused to believe the Germans were invincible and who have fought and who still fight, they've proven it's not so at all, that Germans can be licked, that they are not supermen." He mashed out his cigarette. "Real coffee and real cigarettes—my God, when will we see them again?" He chuckled. "The RAF used to drop us cigarettes. But we had to stop them."

"Why?" Peter asked.

"Can you imagine?"

"No, sir."

"Not so quick, think first."

Peter thought and then shook his head.

"The smell, Peter, the smell. The smell of real tobacco. The smell lingered for a long time. The Nazis arrested people by tracking down the smell."

"That was clever."

"Yes, it was clever. In some things they are clever. The way bloodhounds are clever. Well, I'm off." He stood up, looking as always as though he never was going to stop rising. He ran his hand through Peter's hair and pinched Lise's chin. "Oh, the adoring eyes, the little face, sitting and watching, totally entranced!" He looked at Lise gravely. "Well, all I have to say is that the object of her adoration was in every way worthy." He kissed Lise and left the house.

"Was all that really true?" Peter asked.

"I was only a little girl then," Lise said.

"You mean you've outgrown it?"

Lise smiled and shook her head slowly. "No, Peter, I have not outgrown it. I have never outgrown it." Then she said briskly, "Now brush your teeth and get off to school." He folded his napkin and stood up. She looked at him for a long moment, and then she rose and kissed his cheek. "I'm going to run over and see Mrs. Bertelsen. Have a good day."

He heard the door close as he brushed his teeth. He rinsed his mouth and put on his coat and picked up his briefcase and started down the stairs.

He passed the cellar door. He went to the front door, put his hand on the knob, and then he stopped. He stood there for a moment and then returned to the cellar door. He opened it and looked down.

It was still dark at this early hour. He stood there for a moment, unable to see clearly, and then he flicked on the switch to the cellar light.

He could still see nothing. He walked down the steps, not knowing what he was looking for, what he expected to find, not even really knowing why he was doing this. He went almost to the bottom of the steps and looked around. The cellar was as always, and he felt foolish; now he was half convinced he had never heard voices or seen figures—that it was a dream.

He turned and started quickly up the stairs. Then he stopped. There was something glistening on one of the steps. A spot that caught the light. The spot was red.

His heart started to beat rapidly and his stomach went into a knot.

He bent and touched his finger to the spot. It was sticky.

He rushed up the stairs and into the kitchen and washed the blood from his finger, then leaned against the kitchen sink, breathing hard.

After a few moments he took a sink cloth, wet it, and went back down the stairs and carefully cleaned away the spot. He returned up the stairs, switched off the light, went back to the kitchen and cleaned the cloth.

Then he went to school.

He did not see his father for three days. His mother did not explain where Lars was. Peter knew that his father had to go out of town often for his newspaper, but he did not believe this particular absence had anything to do with the newspaper, the Copenhagen newspaper. But he did not question his mother, and he said nothing of the blood stain on the steps.

6

IN THIS FOURTH CHRISTMAS OF THE OCCUPATION THE DANES had become accustomed to having their unasked German guests in their country. And not even a war, not even the occupation, the Gestapo, the enemy soldiers, could spoil this happy season of the year.

In the Andersen home there were the traditional roast goose and rice porridge. And Lise, as usual, had put enough almonds in the porridge so that all three of them found one in the serving and so was entitled to a present. Of course there was supposed to be only one almond in the porridge, but long ago Lise had changed all that.

There was a small tree, and because decorations were almost impossible to come by now, there were more of the tiny Danish flags fixed on to the branches. Perhaps the scarcity of ordinary decoration was not the entire reason for the profusion of little red flags with their white crosses. That was something for the Germans to see and something the Germans could not object to, even in their present angry mood.

Walking through Snekkersten with his father, Peter

noticed German soldiers staring into the shop windows, all gaily decorated for the holidays. He said to his father they seemed sad.

"Why shouldn't they be sad?" Lars said. "Poor fellows, most of them. They're human too, though what they do tends to make us forget that. Most of them would be just as happy if this war was over and they were back with their families."

That was a new thought for Peter. "But I thought they were the enemy and that they want to conquer the world."

"I doubt most of them feel that way," Lars said. "They've had years of this messy business, and they're probably just as tired of it as everybody else."

"But all the things they've done, the people they've killed."

"I know," Lars admitted. "It's hard to understand, and I'm not even sure I *can* understand it. But many of them are the same as anybody else. They were ordered into the army and ordered to do what they've done. I don't have any love for Germans, Lord knows, but I can't let myself believe that every German is born evil just because he's born German. If I believed that, I would be subscribing to the same stupid philosophy as Adolf Hitler."

"Hitler says it about the Jews," Peter said.

"Hitler says that a people are inherently evil because of their race or religion. Do you know what 'inherently' means?"

"Yes, sir."

"Well, if we believe all Germans are evil then we're agreeing with him in principle, aren't we?"

Peter thought about that for a moment. "I guess so."

38

"They've got a bad track record, no question about that," Lars said. "And they're a tough gang to argue for. But when this business is ended we'll have to live with them, one way or another, and so we must try and see some kind of human decency in them, as difficult as that might be right now."

They paused for a moment and looked at the Sound, choppy with the wind. There was a brief flurry of snow.

"Did you ever hear the expression, 'Vienna Babies'?" Lars asked.

Peter shook his head. "I don't think so."

"Well, after the last war things were very bad in Germany and Austria. The people were starving there. They couldn't feed their children. They shipped thousands of them up here and our families fed them and raised them and they went to Danish schools." Lars hunched deeper into his upturned collar. "They said they would never forget us, that one day they would return. They've returned all right."

They walked past the small Snekkersten inn that in the old days used to be filled with so many tourists and turned up the road leading toward their home.

"But a little while ago you said all Germans couldn't be bad," Peter said.

"I know, I know." Lars sighed. "I'm just as confused as you are. I have certain abstract principles. Do you know what 'abstract' means?"

"Yes."

"I have these principles and I try to live with them, but the Germans confuse me. I have tried all my life to judge people as individuals, not to like or dislike anyone because he is so and so, or such and such. But sometimes the Germans manage to make me dislike them simply because they're Germans. They're to be pitied for that, I suppose. The main thing, though, is that we must all try not to have built-in prejudices. That's the only way we're going to hold this world together."

7

A FEW DAYS LATER PETER WAS REMINDED FORCIBLY OF THIS conversation with his father.

It was the first Wednesday of the New Year, and Wednesday was the day Lars and Lise ran off the little paper. Peter was hurrying home from school to join them and help.

As he hurried along, he saw a crowd gathered in front of the inn. Then he saw the black Gestapo cars. He walked toward the crowd and pushed his way curiously through.

He reached the front of the gathering just in time to see the owner of the inn, Oscar Jensen, a plump, jolly little man, a good friend of Lars, being pushed out of the inn by two Gestapomen. Jensen made no attempt to resist, but the Gestapomen kept jabbing him in the back with their rifles.

Then Peter saw Major Heinz Gruber come out of the inn. The Gestapo chief saw the people gathered in front of the inn and nodded with satisfaction.

Perhaps it was seeing all his friends and neighbors staring at him. Perhaps that had nothing to do with it. But suddenly Oscar Jensen bolted. He ran on his short, fat legs and instinctively the crowd parted to make way for him.

One of the Gestapomen with an automatic rifle cradled in his arms acted equally instinctively. He squeezed the trigger. The bullets came out in a spray. The people screamed, turned, and fled. The innkeeper stumbled, staggered, tried to keep running, fell. There was the silence that follows the sound of shooting.

Peter wet his dry lips. He had never heard an automatic gun fired before, except in American gangster movies.

He looked up as Major Gruber called out, "Stop!"

Peter thought he was ordering the Gestapomen not to fire any more.

"All of you people, stop!" Major Heinz Gruber called out again. He did not shout, yet his voice carried clearly.

The people stopped. They turned and looked at the Germans and at the motionless figure of Oscar Jensen, doubled up on the ground.

"No one will be hurt," Major Gruber said in the same penetrating voice. "But I want all of you to please remain here for a moment."

Peter would never forget that moment. The people of Snekkersten arrested in their flight. One woman sobbing. One man holding his arm where one of the bullets had grazed it. The fat little innkeeper lying on the ground.

Major Gruber walked slowly down the steps of the inn to where Jensen was lying. He looked at the still figure, and then moved his eyes across the faces of the townspeople. A red stain seeped from the body of the innkeeper and turned the snow on the ground a soft pink.

Major Gruber pointed to Jensen. "This man is a traitor," he said.

His Danish was very good. Peter wondered whether

41

this man was one of the Vienna Babies his father had spoken of.

Major Gruber had a kindly expression on his face now. "He is a traitor not to us," he said in a reasonable voice, the voice of a teacher instructing pupils. "I should say he is not a traitor only to us, but a traitor to you as well. He was engaged in illegal activities. He was hurting Denmark by doing so. He was hurting every one of you." He paused and looked benignly at the silent faces. "You have been told many times that we are not here as conquerors but as your protectors, and it is our duty to protect you from your own people as well as from the enemies outside."

He fixed his eyes on the man with the wounded arm. "Do you understand that?" he asked the man. When the man did not answer, he repeated the question.

The man nodded.

"Speak up," Gruber said.

"Yes," the man said.

"If you will come to my headquarters, I will see that you receive medical attention," Gruber said to the man. "I regret that you were in any way hurt by this traitor's stupidity."

Gruber started for his car. As he passed Peter, he paused. He looked at the boy and patted him on the shoulder.

"Do you know what a good friend is, my boy?" he asked Peter.

Peter felt his tongue was stuck in his mouth.

"Answer me, boy," Gruber said in a friendly manner.

Peter could not speak. He felt that clutch in his belly again.

"What is your name, boy?" Gruber asked.

42

Peter managed to get it out. "Peter, sir."

"You must have more name than that," Gruber said jovially.

"Peter Andersen, sir."

"Peter Andersen. A good Danish name. A good Danish Aryan name. You haven't answered me. Do you know what a good friend is?"

"Yes, sir," Peter said.

"Do you believe we are your friends?"

Peter looked around at the people watching him.

"Answer me, Peter, you believe we Germans are your friends?"

Peter looked up at the red face and the small blue eyes. "If you say so, sir," he said.

"You don't believe a German officer would lie, do you?"

"No, sir," Peter said.

"Then if I say we are your friends, you believe that, don't you?"

Peter nodded. "Yes, sir."

Gruber patted his shoulder again. "Remember that," he said. He looked around. "All of you remember that. The Führer believes you are good people, good Aryans. Let us show him that he is not mistaken."

Major Gruber walked to his car. His chauffeur opened the rear door and the major got in. The chauffeur closed the door, got behind the wheel, and drove off. Two Gestapomen picked up Oscar Jensen and carried him into another car. Soon all the Germans were gone.

Slowly the crowd broke up, and the people walked off in all directions. The wounded man, having refused German aid, walked away slowly, holding his arm.

Peter, still shaken from his conversation with the German officer, was one of the last to leave.

He could not take his eyes off the discolored snow. He remembered the stain on the cellar steps.

8

"THE SWINE! THE FILTHY, NAZI SWINE!" LARS ANDERSEN strode back and forth in the living room. Peter had never seen him so angry. He turned furiously on the boy. "What the devil were you doing there, you little fool! You could have got yourself killed!"

"He was just coming home," Lise said tonelessly. She hadn't got angry when she heard what had happened. Her face had turned a deathly white, and Peter thought she was going to faint.

"I'm sorry, son," Lars said. "I'm sorry." He punched the palm of his hand with his fist. "Reflex action. A man runs. You shoot. No orders need be given. It's like a machine. You push a button and something happens. The filthy swine!" He was silent for a moment and then he shrugged. "Well, we can't do anything about it. And the stencil is all made up, so we can't get it into this paper." He snapped his fingers. "The paper! Lise, we're late. We'll have to hurry."

She nodded, and the three of them went down to the basement.

They were working busily when the telephone rang. Lars ran upstairs and answered it. When he walked down the stairs again, his face was grim.

44

Lise looked at him. "Oscar Jensen?"

Lars nodded.

"Is he dead, Father?" Peter asked.

"Yes. But not by bullets."

"But I saw him get shot," Peter said.

"The bullets didn't do the job," Lars said.

"What did it?" Peter asked.

"A ruler," Lars said. He sat down. "A ruler such as you use in school. The kind of ruler you use to measure things and draw straight lines. Do you believe that a man could be killed by a ruler?" He turned to Lise, who had an expression of utter stillness. "Do you, Lise?" Lars breathed heavily. "Oscar was quite alive when they got him to Gestapo headquarters. Weak but alive. The wounds were superficial. Probably the way they were intended to be. The Gestapo is very skillful about those things. He would have recovered. But they started questioning him." Lars Andersen's face hardened. "A charming Nazi euphemism. Do you know what a 'euphemism' is, Peter?"

"No, sir."

Lars smiled in a tired way. "You mean there is actually a word you do not understand?"

"Yes, sir."

" 'Euphemism.' " Lars said. "The substitution of a mild word for another word that might suggest something unpleasant. 'Questioning'—a substitution for beating, torture, for whipping a man across the face with a small, inoffensive ruler, the same as you carry in your briefcase, son, and the metal edge you use to tear paper, cutting into a man's face until it's criss-crossed . . ."

"Lars," Lise said tonelessly.

"He's got to hear these things," Lars said evenly. "I

try to make him understand something about humanity. I tell him there are good, decent Germans. He's got to know about this too."

"He's heard enough," she said.

After a moment Lars nodded and the tension left him. "Yes, I suppose you're right. But something must be done. This cannot just happen."

"And what do you think you can do?" Lise asked. "Are you going to take on the whole Gestapo?"

"Just one man, for the moment. Major Heinz Otto Gruber."

"What can you do?" Lise asked. "What can you do more than you're doing?"

"I don't know. But something must be done. That Nazi swine. Sitting out his country's war like a fat cat on a hearth. I'd like to see him shipped off somewhere where something marvelous could happen to him. Like a Russian bullet through his fat face." Lars leaped to his feet and began to pace back and forth again. "Wouldn't that be something, if we could get him transferred! And under a cloud. A punishment transfer. Wouldn't that be wonderful?"

"How could you do that?" Peter asked.

"I haven't the faintest idea. But something will occur to me, sooner or later."

"Something will occur to you that will have Major Gruber transferred to the Russian front?" Lise asked. And now there was more color to her face and the corners of her mouth were twitching.

Lars flung out his hands. "Russian front, Western front, it doesn't matter. I would just like to see Major Gruber in some unhealthy environment." He bent down and slapped Peter on the knee. "We'll both put our minds to it, son. We'll put the thought into circulation. There must be something unpleasant we can dream up. You'll think, won't you, son?"

Peter grinned. "Yes, Father."

"We'll all think," Lise said drily.

Lars looked at her earnestly. "Don't make fun, Lise. You must not laugh at the power of positive thinking. Thought can move the world. And thought can cope with Major Gruber." He pointed a bony finger at Lise. "You wait and see. We'll think the good major into trouble."

9

TOWARD THE END OF JANUARY, THE WORST KIND OF winter arrived—rain and sleet and the sun never to be seen. Toward the end of that same month, funds for the little paper were running low and there were paper and ink to be bought and new stencils to be found somewhere.

Lars collected money from his fellow newspapermen in Copenhagen, and Lise made the rounds at Snekkersten, asking friends and neighbors to help.

"One woman got so angry," Lise said one evening. She was very tired and wet through and through. "Mrs. Koch. She thinks it's a crime that we put out our little paper."

"She's right. It is," Lars said. He took off Lise's shoes. "Take off your stockings; they're soaked." He got a towel and dried her legs and feet. "Don't be too harsh on poor Mrs. Koch," he said. "She is frightened, that's all. She's just a good, simple human being who's petrified she'll get

47

in trouble just by listening to you. Peter, get your mother's warm slippers. And Mrs. Koch is quite right, you know. By knowing we are getting out our little paper and by not reporting it to the Nazi authorities, she is committing a crime in the eyes of the Germans, and she could be punished severely."

"How do you know she won't report it?" Peter asked, handing his mother the slippers.

"She won't inform because she's a good Dane," Lars said. "She might not have the courage to take any kind of stand against the Germans, even the little stand of contributing a few crowns to an illegal paper, but she is not an informer."

"There are Nazi collaborators," Lise said.

"A few, yes," Lars admitted. "But most of those were always swine, and they have very little to lose."

"There must be Nazi sympathizers among us," Lise said. "By the law of averages there must be a few."

Lars nodded. "I suppose there are some pro-Germans. But that's the chance we must take, and the work must go on." Then he grinned. "You know, I think if any Danes with German sympathies find out what we're doing, they'll be more frightened than anything else."

"Frightened?"

"They know that if the Germans find out about the paper, they'll be the ones suspected, and they know that the Underground will do something about that. And even those swine who have no dislike for Hitler know that there'll be no future in Denmark for informers."

The next day when Peter returned from school he found his mother in bed and Dr. Berg, the family doctor, at her bedside. The doctor greeted Peter and then said, "Your mother is quite ill."

"Nonsense," Lise said.

Peter heard the rasp and tiredness in her voice. "What's the matter with her?"

"She is tired and run down, and she has a chest infection that I don't want to turn into pneumonia. She belongs in a hospital."

"I'll be all right tomorrow," Lise said.

"I'll stop by and have a look at you tomorrow," Dr. Berg said. "And if there is no improvement, it's into the hospital for you." He closed his bag. "Where is Lars?"

"Away," Lise said. "On an assignment."

The doctor glanced at Lise briefly and nodded. "I'll leave a prescription at the apothecary," he said. "Peter, you can pick it up. And Lise, you must remain in bed and keep warm and get some rest. You're on the edge of something serious and at the worst time of the year."

Peter followed the doctor to the apothecary shop and fetched the medicine. He made the dinner for his mother and himself and brought her a tray.

"I have to go out tomorrow," Lise said.

"You can't," Peter said. "You heard what he said."

"I can't help what he said. There are things I must do."

"The paper?"

She nodded, and then she tried suddenly to sit up. "Good heavens! What's happening to my head. I haven't even finished running off the last batch. Peter, help me up."

She tried to get out of bed. He put his hand on her arm. "No, Mother."

She shook her head. "Peter, your father is depending on me. There is one more batch I have to get out and it must be distributed tomorrow."

"The paper can wait," Peter said.

"The paper cannot wait," Lise said.

Peter had never heard quite that tone in his mother's voice. It was weary and hoarse, and yet it had a note in it that accepted no argument.

She gripped his hand. "The paper cannot wait," she repeated. "There are people who live for each edition, each week. It's all they have to go on, to know what's happening. It's almost a way of going to church for some of them. It would disrupt their lives not to get the paper. No matter what Erik Berg says. Peter, that paper must be run off tonight and taken away tomorrow. Now help me."

He helped his mother out of bed and helped her into a warm nightrobe. She leaned on him as they went down to the cellar.

"You have homework," she said.

"I'll help you."

"You'll do your homework. I'm quite all right."

At that moment she leaned against the table and closed her eyes.

"I'm going to help you," Peter said, and he was surprised to find some of the same sound in his own voice. "I'll run off the sheets, and you can stack them."

His mother nodded.

They worked together for more than an hour, Peter cranking the machine, his mother collecting the printed sheets and stacking them. Then Lise leaned back in the chair.

"I'm going to rest, Peter, just for a minute," she said.

She closed her eyes and was asleep.

Peter ran up stairs and brought down a blanket, covered her, and finished the run himself, cranking the machine and stacking the pages. When he was finished, he woke his mother. "I think you'd better get back in bed," he said.

Lise opened her eyes with a start. She shook her head, as though to clear it, and then turned automatically to the machine. She saw that he had finished the job. "I'm sorry, Peter," she said, brushing her hand across her eyes. "I don't know what's the matter with me."

"Dr. Berg knows."

"I can't be bothered with anything as silly as that. Look, Peter, you did it all by yourself. I'm sorry I fell asleep."

Peter wrapped the stack of papers in brown paper and tied it. "There."

"I'll deliver them tomorrow. Thank you, Peter."

He helped his mother back to bed. She seemed very small and frail.

The next morning Lise's condition was worse. She was burning with fever. Peter called the doctor, who spent two minutes with her and then said she must go to the hospital immediately.

"I can't," Lise said.

"You don't have a choice now," the doctor said gently. "It's imperative that you have proper care."

"I cannot go to the hospital," she said.

"Lise," the doctor said. "Believe me when I tell you that this is quite serious."

She shook her head. "I can't, I can't."

But by then the doctor had sedated her and her lovely dark eyes were closing and the only protest was in the shaking of her head. "I can't," she whispered. "I can't."

"I'll call for the ambulance," the doctor said. "Watch her."

When he was gone Lise opened her eyes. "Peter."

"Yes, Mother."

"Don't let him send me to the hospital."

"You have to, Mother."

"Peter, listen to me . . ."

"I know, the paper."

"I have to deliver that package."

"It will have to wait."

"It can't wait. I've explained all that to you." Lise's voice now was getting thick and a little drowsy. She wet her lips and fought to stay awake. "What did he give me?"

"I don't know. He used a needle."

"Oh, God, oh, my God!" She reached out and took his hand. "Peter, I must do something. The paper . . . Your father." She closed her eyes again, and Peter thought she was out, but she forced herself awake again. "Peter, people . . ." She wet her lips again. "Little places, farms . . . all they know is what they see in our little paper. Eyes, ears for them . . . Peter . . ."

He leaned closer to the bed. "Where must it go?" he asked.

She was silent and then she said, "Peter, the paper . . ."

"Where, Mother, where? Where must it be delivered?"

Her eyes opened wider as she suddenly understood

what he was asking and why. "No, no, Peter. Too dangerous. Your father . . ."

"Tell me where, Mother. Where do the packages go?"

She was silent for so long, Peter was certain the sedative now had taken full effect, but then he heard her say in a very low voice, "Near Tivoli, a kiosk."

"I understand, Mother," Peter said.

"Only if a tall, thin woman is there. Only her. Anna. Her name is Anna."

She opened her eyes and peered at Peter, trying to see him. "Not her real name, code . . ." Her eyes closed and her head fell back and she was out.

Dr. Berg entered the room. "It's all arranged, Peter. The ambulance will be here presently. No need for you to wait around. I'll go to the hospital with your mother."

"Yes," Peter said. "Is she very sick, Doctor?"

"She's quite ill, Peter, but once she's in the hospital we'll be able to cope. Now, best you run off to school."

"Yes," Peter said. "Thank you, Doctor."

10

PETER WENT DOWNSTAIRS AND PICKED UP HIS BRIEFCASE, but he did not go out of the house. He went down to the basement and waited. Presently he heard the sound of the ambulance arriving, and he heard the footsteps of the men who came to get his mother. He heard them go upstairs and then come down again and leave the house. And he heard the ambulance leave and then the doctor's car leave and he was alone in the house.

He had been alone before, but this was different. He was in the cellar with several brown parcels tied with string.

He was late for school now, but that didn't matter because he was not going to school that day. He was going to a newspaper kiosk in Copenhagen and he was going to look for a tall, thin woman whose code name was Anna.

The house was very empty. He wondered where his father was and how long he would be away. He suddenly felt young and scared and incompetent. His father was somewhere—he didn't know where—and his mother was in the hospital. And he was alone with parcels of illegal papers that the Germans would like very much to have. Not the papers themselves. They always got copies of the paper. Each weekly edition found its way to the Gestapo desks. And the Germans were always surprised at the accuracy and speed with which events were reported.

No, it was not the parcels they'd want, but information. Who printed it. Where. And at the moment that meant Peter.

The kiosk near Tivoli Gardens. There must be one, only one, or else his mother would have been more specific. A tall, thin woman who would know what he was about when he said the name "Anna."

How best to organize this? How to carry the parcels?

They were just a little more than three inches thick. That was about the thickness of a couple of school books. The briefcase. A schoolboy carrying a briefcase.

Quickly he emptied the briefcase and slipped the

brown paper parcels into it. He snapped the case shut and buckled the straps. It looked quite ordinary.

He started up the steps, and halfway up he thought he'd better hide the books he had removed from the briefcase. The Andersen house had never been honored by a visit from the Germans. But things were not quite the same now. He hid the books behind the furnace, and then he hid the mimeograph machine and the half emptied bottle of ink behind the big furnace as well.

Why would anyone visit—search—the house now? Nothing had really changed. His father was away, as he often was away, and his mother was in the hospital. No one would suspect anything. And yet he felt better for having hid the things—better and a little foolish at the same time.

He looked around. The basement room seemed quite normal—filled with the odds and ends that seem to collect in a basement room.

Holding the briefcase under his arm, pressing it hard against his chest, he went up the stairs, remembering the one that had the blood spot. What had ever happened to that man? Who was he? His parents had never spoken of him.

He switched off the light and shut the cellar door.

He put on his coat and hat and drew on his gloves. Holding the briefcase by its handle, as though it contained nothing but its usual books, he left the house.

The feeling of strangeness persisted. How could the outside of his house, the house he had been born in, seem so different? The street seemed different and every house on it was strange.

He walked carefully so as not to slip on the icy road.

The trees, festooned with icicles, crackled in the wind.

"Peter!"

He stopped short. The call had a crack, like a bullet. He turned toward the building he was passing. A plump woman was standing in the open doorway.

"Hello, Mrs. Bertelsen," he said to his mother's best friend.

"Peter, that ambulance, it came from your direction."

"It's my mother, Mrs. Bertelsen," he said.

"Good gracious, Peter, what's the matter with her?"

"Chest infection. Dr. Berg was afraid it might turn into pneumonia."

"Oh, the poor thing. This weather. Your mother doesn't take care of herself, Peter. Rushing around all the time and getting overtired, and we're none of us getting proper food these days, are we?"

"No, I guess not, Mrs. Bertelsen." He tried to edge on.

"Is there anything I can do?"

"No, ma'am, thank you."

"Did you have a good breakfast?"

"Yes, ma'am."

"One must eat properly. The weather. Your poor mother."

He started off again.

"Peter."

"Yes, ma'am."

"You and your father. You must eat with us tonight."

"My father is away. I don't know when he'll be back."

"Then you're all alone?"

"Yes, ma'am."

"Poor child, all the more reason for you to come here."

"Yes, ma'am."

She stepped back into the house, and he hurried on.

11

PETER BOUGHT HIS TICKET AND WALKED OUT ONTO THE station platform. A group of German soldiers was waiting for the Copenhagen train. They stood in the middle of the platform, talking loudly.

Peter sat down on a bench and placed the briefcase upon his knees. He stiffened slightly as he saw two of the German soldiers leave the group and walk toward him.

He didn't think he looked suspicious, and yet he felt that knot in his stomach again, and his heart began to beat harder and faster. He was just an ordinary Danish schoolboy, he told himself, with an ordinary Danish schoolboy's briefcase on his knees. He told himself there were thousands and thousands of them in Denmark. Nothing out of the ordinary.

He watched the soldiers come closer.

But there was something. Ordinary Danish schoolboys were in ordinary Danish schools at this hour of the day and were not sitting on benches in railroad stations waiting for a train.

The briefcase on his knees seemed to double in size.

The soldiers paused as they passed him. He started to shake. He tried not to look at them, tried not to not look at them.

"Hello, there," one of the soldiers said in passable Danish.

Peter raised his eyes. He saw the soldiers were quite young, hardly older than boys.

"Hello, young man," the same soldier said.

"Hello, sir," Peter said.

"It's cold, not?"

"Yes," Peter said.

"Is that why you shiver?"

"Yes."

The other soldier broke into a smile. "But a healthy young boy, the cold is not too cold, yes?"

Peter nodded. "It's cold."

"It is because you sit in the one place," the first soldier said. "When it is cold it is good to march. Marching fast and the cold is no longer so cold, no?"

"I guess so, sir."

"Good." The soldier clapped Peter on the shoulder. "Then march. It is good for you, and it will give you experience when you become a soldier."

Peter stood up. The briefcase fell to the platform.

One of the soldiers picked it up and handed it back to him. "Your hands are cold, not? Walk quickly and everything will warm up."

"One, two, one, two," the other soldier said.

Clutching the case tightly, Peter began to walk down the platform.

"Straighten up," one of the soldiers called out. "Shoulders back, belly in."

Peter squared his shoulders and tried to march in a military manner. He was glad his back was to the soldiers. When he reached the end of the platform he turned. The two soldiers were close behind him. He felt himself panicking again. The soldiers waved good-naturedly to him and went into the men's toilet.

A few moments later the train pulled in. Peter got into the nearest car. Just before the doors shut, he saw the two soldiers running out of the toilet. Another soldier held a door open for them.

Peter stood on the platform at the end of the car and looked down through the car. The train had started its run at Elsinore and was not yet crowded with the passengers it would pick up on the way to Copenhagen.

There were the usual passengers, soldiers, of course, businessmen, women. One type of passenger he did not see. He saw no other boy of school age carrying a briefcase.

He stood on the platform a moment longer. It was important where he took a seat. It also was important that he not remain too long on the platform with all the empty seats in the car.

The seats, as on all those trains, were divided between those that ran lengthwise and those that faced each other. He saw a smallish, gray-haired woman seated half way down the car. She was looking out of the window. He walked down and took the seat opposite her. He settled in the seat and put the briefcase on his lap. His heart was still beating fast.

The train moved slowly out of the station. The lovely winter Danish countryside moved by. The trees glittered with ice.

Peter stared straight ahead. Presently he was conscious of the fact that the woman was gazing at him. He turned to her and smiled politely.

"Good morning," she said. She had a faint accent.

"Good morning, ma'am," he said.

She gestured with her head. "It is so pretty outside."

"Yes, ma'am."

"Where do you live?"

"In Snekkersten."

"Ah, yes, I have been there. It is very pretty."

She looked out the window again, and then she unfolded a newspaper. Peter was relieved that she would read and not ask him questions. He leaned back in his seat and looked out of the window, and then his eye was caught by the paper as she unfolded it, and he saw the big Gothic letters *Völkischer Beobachter*. That was German, he knew, and now he also knew the woman's accent.

His first impulse was to move to another car, but he realized immediately how stupid that would be. Besides, she was just a German woman reading a German newspaper. But he wished he had picked another seat, oh, he wished that.

He heard the woman speak again. "Are you going to Copenhagen?"

Peter nodded. His mouth was too dry to speak. Then he thought how stupid that was. He could have named any town, the next town, and had an excuse to get off the train. But he didn't have to get off the train.

"Is that where your school is?" she asked, looking at the briefcase.

"No, ma'am."

She looked at him knowingly. "You are not going to school today."

After a moment he shook his head.

"Naughty boy," she said, smiling. "Do your parents know you are playing truant today?"

He shook his head again.

The woman chuckled. "You must not do this very often. You look quite guilty."

He tried for a smile.

"It is the same with all children, I suppose. But it is not a good thing to do too often."

"I don't," he said.

"I can tell." She laughed. It was a merry, tinkling laugh. "I have never seen anyone look so guilty. You must be a very good boy." She leaned over and patted his knee. "Never to mind. Boys will be boys. But you must not make this a habit. Without school you will grow up uneducated, and that is bad. Do you agree?"

"Yes, ma'am."

"This time I will not tell your parents." She laughed again at her own humor. "What will you do with yourself in Copenhagen?"

She pronounced it like all the Germans, with a soft "a," as though it was spelled Copenhahgen.

Why wasn't Tivoli open, he asked himself. That would have been an easy excuse. What could he tell her? What would a schoolboy do in Copenhagen in the middle of the winter? "I'm going to a museum," he said.

"A museum?" The woman nodded approvingly. "That is not too bad then. You will not waste your day. Which museum?"

He tried to think. His father had taken him to several at one time and another.

"Which museum do you have in mind?" the woman asked again.

It was Peter's first attempt at sustained lying, and he was not finding it easy.

He remembered one. "The National Museum."

"Oh, yes, the National Museum. I have been there several times. It is a good, interesting place. Folk history is very important, don't you agree?"

"Yes, ma'am."

"It is the substance of a country, the people, the folk."

He noticed a slight change in her voice.

She pointed to the newspaper. "The Leader's own paper," she said. "How shall I translate the name for you? 'The Peoples' Observer.' You see, the folks' observer. The Leader believes more in the German folk than in anything else. You have heard that?"

Peter nodded.

"It is what he says all the time, 'One folk and one Leader.'" Her voice now was filled with mysticism. "Have you ever heard our Leader speak?"

"Yes, ma'am."

She smiled warmly. "Perhaps you are doing a wise thing after all, to stay away from school and the false teachings there, and to find the real truth in the history of your people. If I had the time, I would happily spend the day with you."

She turned to the window. They were passing the deep woods that bordered the deer park. "I have spent three years here now. But now I must return to the Fatherland, and I look forward so much to that. Have you ever been in Germany, young man?"

"No, ma'am."

"It is the most beautiful country in the world. Some day after the war when we are all one people, you will visit and you will see."

She resumed reading the paper, and Peter was grateful

it held her attention until the train reached Copenhagen. She looked up as the train slowed, entering the Central Station. She held out the paper. "Take this. It is always fine to read, but this particular issue has a speech made by the Führer. Read it and whatever parts of it you understand will teach you. What is your name, young man?"

"Peter."

"The Führer would love you, Peter. He loves young people." She held out her hand. "It was pleasant to meet you, Peter."

"Thank you, ma'am."

The car was very crowded now and they had to wait to get out and she smiled at him and the briefcase pulled on his arm. Once they stepped out of the car onto the platform, she began to stride purposefully, ignoring the people all around her, and soon she outdistanced Peter. When she reached the steps, she turned back and waved her hand in farewell.

As Peter made his way to the steps, he was suddenly aware of the fact that he had in one hand packets of illegal, Underground papers, and in the other, the official newspaper of Adolf Hitler.

When he could, without attracting attention, he slipped the German newspaper into a trash bin.

12

PETER STOOD IN THE MAIN HALL OF THE STATION FOR a moment or two to get his bearings.

The Central Station in Copenhagen was the largest in the country, but vast as it was, it was thronged day and night. There were German soldiers everywhere in Denmark these days, especially at railroad stations; they always seemed to be moving here and there, but there were more Germans in the Central Station than anywhere else, and it was not only because it was so large.

For this station was the railroad hub of the country. From it trains went everywhere. They went north through northern Sealand. They went across the Great Belt to the middle island of Funen, beloved by the Danes because it contained the city of Odense where Hans Christian Andersen was born, and then continued on across the Little Belt to Jutland, the westernmost part of Denmark and the part connected with Germany. But most important for the Germans, trains went south from Copenhagen, down southern Sealand, and finally reached the ferry crossing over to Warnemünde in Germany.

Standing there, listening to the babble of voices around him, voices in German, voices in Danish with every accent in the land, Peter again felt a wave of fear. There were so many of them. The soldiers didn't bother him so much. They were coming and going, with their rifles and haversacks, and didn't have much time or interest to wonder about a schoolboy with a briefcase. But all the men in civilian clothes. The men in the dark suits and dark hats who lounged around as though they had nothing in the world on their minds, and whose eyes were as sharp as ferrets, watching, watching. The men with the manner that had come to be known as the Gestapo manner. Were any of them observing him? Were any of them wondering what a Danish schoolboy was doing away from school at that hour of the morning?

For a moment he had an almost uncontrollable urge

to turn around and go back to the platform and catch the next train back to Snekkersten. To get back home and get rid of the packets of papers. They would be gone in the furnace in less than five minutes.

Then he felt ashamed of himself. He remembered the hours spent working on the machine, getting out the sheets of paper which one moment were blank, meaningless, nothing, and the next, carried words written by his father. Words that men risked their lives to learn; words that were read by hundreds, thousands of people; words that brought hope and faith and the strength to face the day and tomorrow's day and the day after that.

Some of that was in his hands now, and he thought of his father, and he thought of his mother pushing the bicycle loaded down with paper and how small she was, and a woman at that, and how she faced the Germans every day and she was still able to smile.

Peter gripped the handle of the case and glanced around again. The station restaurant was filled; there was a long line in front of the station kiosk, and he was glad that was not the one where he had to drop off the packet. Then he walked resolutely out of the main entrance. There were all kinds of strange men walking about, or leaning against the walls, and he tried not to look at them and hoped they were not looking at him.

He walked out of the station, crossed the street, passed the entrance to the Terminus Hotel, his father's favorite in Copenhagen, and he remembered being taken there by his father and mother for dinner many times. He turned left at the corner and walked down to the busy Vesterbrogade, crowded even these days with traffic, trams, military cars, taxis.

He turned right on Vesterbrogade and felt his heart begin to beat faster. It was getting near the time now. He walked past a store, past a restaurant, past more stores, past a bar, past the beginning of Tivoli Gardens, past the main entrance to Tivoli, past Tivoli, past another restaurant, and then beyond that, just beyond that, he saw a small arcade and at the front of the arcade a kiosk, and that must be the kiosk. He was almost there and now he was there and he walked past the kiosk not only because he just couldn't bring himself simply to walk up to it but because out of the corner of his eye he saw someone inside the kiosk—and it was not a tall, thin woman.

He kept walking until he came to the corner that faced Town Hall Square. The sidewalk tables at Frascati's had been removed for the winter, and the restaurant looked abandoned. It was crowded inside, as always, but somehow it never looked fully dressed without the tables outside.

The wind blew across the open square. The pigeons were there in the little park opposite the Town Hall, but not many people came at this time of year to feed them. There were three or four little *polse* wagons about and people in front of them eating sausages. The pigeons gathered there, hoping the people would throw them bits and pieces of uneaten rolls. And of course the people did. Food might not be the magnificent triumph it ordinarily was in Denmark, but there was enough, and there was always some for the pigeons. For the pigeons, of course, owned the little park and allowed people to go there only on sufferance.

Peter did not know exactly what to do. He guessed there was an exact time that the packet should be delivered, and he knew that if his mother had not been so dopey with the sedation, she would have given him the time. No she would not. If she had not been so drugged, she wouldn't have allowed him to be doing this at all.

In any case, he could not stand there on the street corner, looking like a country bumpkin, looking even more like a lost schoolboy, attracting attention, attracting questions. He waited for the light to change. Then he crossed the street and walked in front of the Town Hall and down the Stroeget, the little narrow street with its shops that were so marvelous in the good days and which still were, especially to the Germans, quite wonderful.

Even in the cold the street was filled. There were many soldiers, some of them with Danish girls, although not very many, most of them walking in twos and threes, looking in windows. Peter walked down as far as the old church, and then he turned around and started back. Perhaps the tall, thin woman would be there now.

As he approached the kiosk again, he felt a tingle of excitement. But this time his heart was not pounding as it had before, and he did not know whether it was because he was getting a little braver or whether it was just that he was cold and wanted to get rid of the packet and go home.

As he came to the kiosk, he saw there was a tall, thin woman behind the counter this time. There were a couple of customers, buying papers. He wanted to glance up and down the street, but then he thought that would be a dead giveaway, and anyway, what would he be looking for, so he walked up to the kiosk and got behind a man who was paying for a magazine. He unstrapped the briefcase and snapped open the clasp, and after the man ahead of him started off, he put the briefcase on the counter with the open end toward the woman and asked for a copy of a boys' illustrated magazine.

He pointed. "That one, Anna."

The woman made no sign that the name meant anything to her. She turned her back to Peter without looking at him and took the magazine he had asked for out of the rack. Then as she turned back to him, she bent over and picked up a stack of newspapers and covered the briefcase.

She told him how much the magazine cost, and when he paid her, she opened the till below the counter. She reached into the till with one hand and under the stack of papers with the other. She gave Peter his change, rearranged the papers on the counter, pushed his briefcase toward him, and asked the next customer what he wanted. Peter saw that the briefcase was empty.

He thanked the woman, slipped the case off the counter and under his arm, and started off, holding the magazine in his other hand. He was about twenty-five feet from the kiosk when he heard sounds of a commotion. He turned his head. Two men were pushing the customer who had followed him to one side and were talking in loud voices to the tall, thin woman.

Both men were dressed in black coats and hats and Peter heard the accent, the hated accent, and he started to walk away fast, then faster, and then he heard a shout behind him, and the word, "Halt!" And it was spoken with the same hated accent.

Now he started to run. People on the crowded street looked at him curiously, and again he heard the harsh command "Halt!" and he ran faster, holding the briefcase and the magazine, wondering where he could go, how long it would be before they caught him.

68

He twisted his head. He could make out the man running after him. He wondered why the man was still so far away. And then he saw that people in the street were somehow getting in the way of the German pursuing him.

Without knowing anything about anything, the people on the street saw a man running after a boy, and they heard him shouting to the boy in a German accent. That was enough. In one way or another they managed to slow up the German. He kept pushing the people aside and shouting to the boy to halt.

Peter kept running as fast as he could, wondering how long his wind would hold out, remembering crazily at that moment how his father had been a great track star and how his mother used to sit and watch him, and he felt his breath grow short and sharp and cut across his throat like a razor.

He slipped on a patch of ice. He felt his knee hit the ground painfully and then he felt a hand grasp him and bring him to his feet and he ran on without knowing who it was who helped him.

He saw he was in front of Tivoli Gardens again. The park was gray and dark and silent, but the gates were open because of maintenance work that was going on inside. The last time he had been in Tivoli was with his mother and father one happy Sunday evening in August.

Peter ran into the park. A Danish attendant sat behind one of the windows where, in the summer, tickets were sold. He started to say something, and then he too somehow understood and he merely looked on silently as the boy ran past him. Once inside, Peter looked around, trying to decide where to go.

Tivoli looked quite different in January. The buildings where the pantomimes were performed, where the concerts were played, the restaurants, the little stands that sold sausages and beer and soda and ice-cream, the amusement stands—all were closed, the windows boarded.

As he kept running, almost out of breath now, Peter felt a sense of unreality, of ghostliness, in this lovely and familiar place. So many of the happy memories of his young life were mixed up with Tivoli—always lights and music and people laughing, even after the Germans came. But now it was a Tivoli in a kind of nightmare; empty, soundless, unpeopled, on a dark, gray winter day. There were not even the echoes of the laughter and the music.

Unpeopled. Unpeopled, yes, except for the people seeking him.

He ran one way and then another; came to a small lake and ran round it, realized he was headed back in the same direction from which he had come, stopped and leaned against a tree, breathing hard. He heard the sounds of heavy footsteps and of heavy voices, so there now was more than one, and he heard the shout again, "Halt!" But he did not think anyone actually saw him at the moment, and in any case he was halted, leaning against the tree.

He remembered seeing a film once about England in the last century. Hounds were chasing a fox, and he remembered the face of the fox in the picture, the eyes, and now he was the fox. He wondered whether the Germans would get dogs. They often used bloodhounds to track people down.

He heard the footsteps come closer, and he knew he had to move. He ran toward the part of the pleasure park with the amusements. His lungs felt as though they were going to explode. The briefcase seemed filled with bricks, empty as it was. He thought about dropping it, but it had his name on it. He wondered how many Peter Andersens there were in Denmark. But then he thought that the Germans would question the woman at the kiosk, and it would help them if they had a name to thrust upon her.

Then he remembered something else, something his father had told him. He had asked Lars about people getting caught and tortured and giving away names and his father had explained that in the Underground people generally knew only the names of one or two other persons with whom they worked. The woman at the kiosk probably didn't know the name of Lars Andersen. Peter started to throw away the briefcase and then decided not to. They might be able to trace something.

He ran past the amusement place with the small colliding automobiles, remembering how he and his father used to love to go there and smack into each other in the little cars. Who ever would have believed that the next time he would be there he would be running away from the Gestapo?

He knew he couldn't go much farther. He rested for a moment against the guard wall of the miniature auto arena. His breath tore his throat. Despite the freezing cold, the sweat was streaming down his face and his back felt wet and cold.

Again he heard the pounding footsteps and the talking in German, and he ran from the place with the little cars, now all covered with canvas and huddled like tiny animals in one part of the arena, until he saw that he was in front of the huge ferris wheel. He paused and looked around. He could hear the running feet, but he could not see anyone.

71

He ran to one of the gondolas on the ferris wheel. He twisted the handle and the door opened and he climbed into it and crouched down on the floor.

The footsteps seemed to get closer. Then there was silence. He remained there, huddled on the floor, breathing hard, wondering why they couldn't hear that heavy breathing. It seemed anyone in the whole of Tivoli should be able to hear it.

It seemed a long time. He could hear nothing now. He started to raise his head to look over the door sill when he heard the voices, and he ducked his head quickly. He heard the footsteps and then their sound got fainter and he raised his head again and looked over the sill and saw two men walking away. He watched them go, his breath coming easier again, and then he saw a third man, smoking a cigarette, and fortunately for Peter, looking in another direction. Again Peter ducked down, and again he could feel a new pounding in his heart.

He waited again. Again he carefully raised his head. The man was gone. There was no one in sight. Had they gone? Were they just hiding, waiting?

Then he heard the voices again, and they seemed quite far away. He dropped down from the gondola. He looked one way and then another. The place seemed truly deserted. He moved carefully toward the rear of Tivoli, where he knew there was an exit opposite the Glyptotek Museum.

He turned a curve in the walk and froze. A man was standing near the exit gate. His back was toward Peter. He could not tell what he was. He was dressed in dark clothes. Peter slipped behind a tree and waited.

A moment later another man joined the first man, and they spoke to each other. Peter was grateful for the

German habit, so laughed at by Danes, of talking loudly at all times, shouting almost, even though they were close to each other. It was easy for Peter to hear that the language they were speaking was not Danish.

He backed away slowly and hid behind another tree. He was trapped now. They knew about that back exit. They must know about all the exits. He was trapped, the way the fox was trapped in that picture.

He wished his father were there. As impossible as it seemed, he knew his father would be able to figure some way out. But whatever that would be, it was beyond him, and he thought the simplest thing to do was to give himself up. Maybe they wouldn't be so hard on a boy his age.

Then he heard another sound, the clip-clop of horse's hooves. He turned toward the sound and saw a small wagon, filled with cut branches. A Danish workman held the reins of the horse. He saw Peter and Peter saw him. The man beckoned. Peter ran to the wagon. The man nodded toward the rear. Peter climbed onto the back of the wagon, separated the cut branches and twigs and crawled underneath them. He felt himself being covered with the pieces of trees, and then everything went dark as a tarpaulin was spread on top of the branches.

The wagon started moving. So slowly. The horse's hooves seemed to be in slow motion. Peter lay stretched prone on the wagon bed and felt the jolting of the wheels and listened to the clip, clop, clip, clop, and thought that by now they surely could have crossed half of Sealand. Then he heard the voice, and it was the first voice, the voice that he had heard at the kiosk, and it said the same thing, "Halt!" Only this time it was close, inches away it seemed. And the wagon stopped.

"Have you seen a boy here?" the voice asked in terrible Danish, and what was terrible was that it was so near.

He heard the voice of what must have been the wagon driver, "I don't understand you."

"A boy. A young boy, with a briefcase. Did you see him?"

"I have been trimming trees."

"Did you see such a boy?"

"No."

"You are sure?"

"I do not understand."

The German said something angrily in his own language, and the wagon started moving again. It stopped and started and then it stopped again, and the tarpaulin was pulled aside. The wagon driver helped pull away the branches, and Peter crawled out. He saw he was in the part of the city near one of the artificial lakes.

"Thank you," Peter said to the driver. "Thank you."

The wagon driver finished spreading the tarpaulin. He climbed up to his seat and picked up the reins. "I never saw you," he said. The wagon moved on.

Peter started for the Vesterport station.

13

"YOU DID NOTHING WRONG," LARS SAID.

This was the fifth time he had said it, and Peter was not yet convinced.

"I must have," he said. "I must have been stupid in some way."

"You were not stupid," Lars said patiently.

The father and son were standing at the ramparts of Hamlet's castle, staring out at the roiling water of the Kattegat where it stormed into the narrow mouth of the Sound.

Peter and his father had visited Lise in the hospital in Elsinore. She had won her battle with the germs and would soon be released. After leaving the hospital they had wandered over to the old Kronborg Castle, which in its somber vastness seemed to speak a silent message of another Denmark, of another day.

"They simply had their eye on that kiosk and were waiting," Lars said.

"I should have been more careful," Peter insisted.

"Careful? How could you have been more careful? You had no instructions other than to deliver the papers. I would have done the same thing and probably would have been caught."

"But I should have noticed the Gestapoman."

"You undoubtedly did see him, just as you saw many others," Lars said. "Unless the Gestapo is in uniform or is shouting or torturing someone, they look quite like other human beings. And the Germans pick rather ordinary looking men for this kind of work. They'd be useless, wouldn't they, if they had 'Gestapo' stamped on their neat, dark coats?"

"What do you think will happen to that woman, the one in the kiosk?"

"I don't know. I don't think too much."

"They'll try to make her talk."

"Yes."

Lars paused in front of one of the old cannon which in older days used to lob cannon balls into the air to drop on foreign vessels whose masters, in a temporary state of stupidity, had failed to pay the tolls exacted by the Danish lords. It was considered amateurish just to fire a round into the ship. The drill was to aim the cannon ball into the sky and have it drop like a basketball.

"Yes," Lars repeated. "They'll try to make her talk, and they'll cause some pain before they realize she knows nothing."

"She doesn't know you, then?" Peter asked.

Lars shook his head. "No, she does not know me. She might recognize your mother, but she doesn't know her name. All she knows is that someone brings the papers there and that soon afterward, normally, someone else takes them away. She is an old woman and a brave woman, and perhaps even the Gestapo will realize before they do too much damage that she is only a connection in the chain and has nothing actually to do with the paper."

They walked along the path in front of the old castle. There were German guards posted where Danish guards used to mount their station of honor. Where the Danish guards had no real function, other than to evoke old memories and see that children didn't hurt themselves crawling over things, the Germans on guard were told they were defending the Fatherland, and many of them believed it.

Peter shrank back instinctively when he saw the German uniform. Lars put his hand on his son's shoulder and squeezed it reassuringly.

When Peter had first told his father what had happened to him, Lars had turned white. He questioned Peter carefully and at great length before the color came back to his face and his voice became normal. Then Peter had said it might be dangerous for him to go out of the house, that the Gestapo might still be looking for him.

"Did they see your face?" Lars had asked.

"I don't think so," Peter said.

"It must be better than that," Lars said harshly. "Think. Think carefully. Did they ever actually see your face?"

After a while Peter shook his head. "No, Father."

"You are sure?"

"Yes, Father."

"Think carefully, son."

"They never were that close," Peter said.

Lars breathed out hard. "Good. Then I think you have little to worry about. So many boys your age look alike. It would be more dangerous, perhaps, if you changed any of your ordinary ways."

"Father," Peter said after a moment.

"Yes, son."

"What if they had seen my face?"

"You would be in Sweden before morning," Lars had said.

After that they had agreed not to tell Lise, and they had gone to the hospital.

"That woman, the one at the kiosk," Peter said again.

"What about her?" Lars asked.

"Will you be able to find out what happens to her?"

"I think so." Lars turned his eyes away from the sea and gazed at his son. "You are growing up, Peter."

"Of course I am, Father."

"I like the way you are growing up," Lars said.

Peter turned away, his throat filling.

"We have spoken of the old woman at the kiosk," Lars said. "We have not yet finished speaking about you."

"You asked me everything, again and again," Peter said.

"I asked what happened to you."

"It was exciting," Peter said. "They didn't have a chance."

"I'm sure," Lars said in his dry voice. Then he asked, casually, "Why did you do it?"

"Why did I run away? Gosh . . ."

"Not run away. Why did you deliver the papers?"

"Why, you know . . . Mother couldn't . . ."

"Yes, I know she couldn't. Why did you do it then?"

"Well, she explained to me how important it was."

"How important, Peter?" Lars asked. "Important to whom?"

"She said it was very important to you." He looked up at his father anxiously. "You mustn't be angry with mother for letting me do it. She was half asleep with that stuff the doctor gave her. She didn't know what she was saying."

"I'm not angry with her," Lars said with a small smile. "Did she say the paper was important only to me?"

"Oh, no! To everybody who reads it. She said it was one of the things that keeps them going, that they couldn't do without it . . ." He raised his eyes. "They'll have to do without it this time, won't they, Father?"

"No, more papers were run off. They were delivered to another place and distributed to the people." He looked thoughtfully at Peter. "And did that mean something to you, the fact that many people depended on the paper?"

"Yes, Father."

"Are you sure you understand? I want you to think carefully about this. 'Man does not live by bread alone.' Matthew, more or less. The bread is important, and from that point of view we are not having a difficult time of it here in Denmark, compared to other places. But it isn't enough just to eat and not have to hide from bombs."

They paused as two German guards marched past, and then continued on.

"I give thanks every day that our little country has been spared real fighting," Lars went on. "And yet there is a kind of purity in danger and suffering. When Mr. Churchill said this was Britain's finest hour, he was speaking the simple truth. Those poor people, suffering, dying, their cities being destroyed. But they must feel very pure inside. They know that in enduring, in simply not surrendering, they are putting down things in history that will never be forgotten."

He was silent as they walked, and then he said, "We don't have that. But we did an important thing. We took a stand. It took us almost four years, but at last we took a stand."

"With the Danish Jews?"

"Yes, starting with them. It was nothing that will change the history of the world, but it may in some way change our history. It was immoral to round up and kill those Danes and our people could not tolerate that and we did something. And that's the important thing. Not the size of armies and battles. But in the face of their soldiers and Gestapo and tanks and guns and planes we stood up and said you will not do this evil thing, and we stopped them from doing it. The only country in Europe, Peter, the only country to save almost its entire Jewish community.

"Those poor people became our conscience in a way, and now they're over there, across that little stretch of water, and they can see Denmark as we can see Sweden. The younger ones are joining a Danish Brigade and making plans to return to their homeland. And they will return and we will welcome them." He put his hand on Peter's shoulder. "Later on, when you're older and reading all about these times as history, you need not feel ashamed of your little country."

"That's why your paper is so important," Peter said.

"You understand that?" Lars said. "Yes, that's why the little paper is so important. It is another stand. It's another small stand, but all our contributions are quite small, and we must cherish every one of them."

They turned and started back toward town.

"That was the importance of delivering those papers, Peter," Lars said. "I'm grateful nothing more serious happened to you, but if it had, it would not have been meaningless."

14

"AS A MATTER OF FACT," LARS SAID, "IT WAS RATHER marvelous. No woman around to nag us. Correct, Peter?"

"Correct," Peter said heartily.

"Eat what we liked. When we liked. It was almost like being on a hunting trip. Correct, son?"

"Correct!"

Lise looked around. "I see what you mean. The place looks like a camp. A camp in the jungle. When was that ashtray emptied last? Whose shoes are those, yours, Lars? Or yours, Peter? Look at this kitchen. It looks as though a cyclone hit it."

"Women," Lars sighed. "Peter, let this be a living lesson to you. Remember how quiet and happy it's been around here for the last week. And see how it is now, ten minutes after your mother gets back from the hospital. Lise, couldn't they have kept you there a little longer?"

The three of them looked at each other and then all burst into laughter. Lars threw his arms around Lise and started to dance her around the room and then remembered she was just out of sick bed, and he stopped and just held her very tightly.

"And now," she said. "Tell me the truth. How have you two scoundrels got along?"

"Fantastically," Lars said.

"Marvelously," Peter said.

"Well, fairly well," Lars said.

"Not too bad," Peter said.

"To tell the truth, rotten!" Lars shouted.

"Terrible!" Peter yelled.

Lise smiled. She looked pale and tired, but her eyes glowed. "I think everybody should go into hospital every now and then. I'd forgotten how much I loved our little house and how pretty it is."

"We tried to keep it clean," Peter said.

"It is clean and beautiful and you're both beautiful and I feel beautiful and it's beautiful to be home."

"Take advantage of this mood," Lars informed Peter. "It won't last very long."

With Lise back and after a few days her old self again, the Andersen household returned to normal, normal for that time. The paper was run off on its appointed day and sent to the proper places. What had happened to Peter was kept from Lise, as agreed, but one evening Lars told Peter privately that the old woman from the kiosk had been released by the Germans and had not had too hard a time of it.

About a week after Lise's return, another mysterious visitor was spirited into the house by Pastor Holm. This time he was brought to the house while Peter was awake and saw everything.

The man seemed to be in his middle twenties. His face might have been pleasant, ordinarily, or it might have been anything, but at the moment no one could tell. It was out of shape as a result of Gestapo interrogation. His right hand was bandaged.

His name didn't matter, the priest said. "He is like you, Lars, the publisher of a small paper. That is all you need to know."

Peter looked wonderingly at Pastor Holm. He had known him all his life, and he never would have guessed that he would be doing the things he did. Pastor Holm was the little church and a sermon on Sundays and people getting married and buried. But he also was a man who took in people wounded and injured and damaged in their fight for Denmark and he helped them get to safety.

Now, the big priest with his rosy cheeks and his bright, clear blue eyes was looking at the stranger with pretended disgust. "Look at him," he said in his deep, pulpit voice. "Look at that fool. He's still laughing at what he did. It almost cost him his life, and if we don't get him out of the country soon, the Gestapo will find him again and finish what they started. But he still laughs."

"Nothing the matter with laughing," Lars said.

"No, of course not," Holm boomed. "You're just as crazy as he is. It's why I brought him here. Birds of a feather."

The five of them were in the basement. The curtains had been drawn, and the only light was from a flickering candle. Lise had prepared a meal for the stranger, and he age it hungrily, if painfully.

"You're really starved," Peter said.

"After three months in Vestre prison as it's operated by the Germans, I think I shall always be hungry," the man said.

Peter couldn't take his eyes from the man's face. The candlelight seemed to add to the distortion. The man caught him staring at him and burst into laugher again.

"It's a funny face, isn't it, son?"

Peter flushed. "I'm sorry, sir."

"Not at all. Would you believe that until three months ago there were pretty girls who thought I was handsome?"

"Yes, sir," Peter said firmly.

"Good boy. Good lie, but good boy. But it's quite true, son. I wasn't a movie idol, you understand, but I had no trouble with the girls. But look at me now! You see, that's what comes from keeping bad company. And take my word, the Gestapo is the worst company in the world."

"Because you're such a bloody fool," Pastor Holm snorted.

The strange man had a couple of glasses of aquavit and ate more food that Lise brought down from the kitchen. What had happened to him, he said as he finished the last of the cold meat, was quite funny.

"Very funny," Holm said.

"Can you tell us what it was?" Peter asked. "I'm sorry. I guess it's a secret."

"I don't know from whom, now," Pastor Holm said. "That's the whole point." He turned to the man. "Go ahead. Tell them your foolish story. It will make them laugh and help pay for your supper."

The man drained another glass of aquavit and wiped his lips. "Well, it was this way: I was walking alongside the quay, just near the Christiansborg Palace. All of a sudden I found a strange man walking alongside me. At first I thought it was just that someone was happening to walk at the same rate of speed I was. But when I slowed he slowed, and when I walked faster he walked faster. And then I knew it was no coincidence, and since no Dane would be guilty of such bad manners, I knew he had to be a German. And since he was in ordinary clothing, he had to be the Gestapo. You see, young man, the power of deduction."

Again the priest snorted.

"We walked along, and I wondered when he would start his conversation. I knew there would be a conversation or else I would have already been arrested. Gestapo-men do not stroll streets for no reason," the man said.

"Power of deduction," Pastor Holm said derisively.

"Well, finally my friend opened up," the stranger continued. "What it was was simply this: would I turn informer?"

Peter's eyes widened. He was sitting on the floor, his arms wrapped around his legs, and his eyes got as large as saucers.

"Yes, son, he offered me a hundred crowns just to consider working for the Gestapo, and another nine hun-

84

dred crowns if I agreed," the man said, talking directly to the boy. "We were having trouble with the paper; we needed money badly, so I took the hundred crowns and said that I would think it over."

"And so you should have," the priest said angrily. "And let it go at that. You were a hundred crowns richer, and your face was your own."

"Yes, that's what everybody said," the man admitted. "But the paper needed money very badly."

"We know about that," Lars said.

"Besides, I considered the German mentality. You see, if it had been the British Secret Service, I would have been arrested. The British would have been quite content to have the head man. But the Germans, I knew, were different. They are more thorough, always. They would be satisfied only if they could arrest the entire apparatus. So as long as I left off mentioning names, I was safe, I thought."

"You thought," Holm said. "That was another mistake."

"Well, I went back to where the Gestapoman had told me to meet him, and I told him I accepted his offer," the man said. He held out his glass. Lars filled it again with aquavit. The man drank it off in one swallow. He looked at the empty glass for a moment. "He gave me the nine hundred crowns and we shook hands over a glass of snaps, like this." He held up the glass. "Have you ever shaken hands with a Gestapoman and had a drink with him?" he asked the room.

Lars shook his head. "I have not yet been so honored."

"You must try it sometime," the man said. "It's quite

extraordinary. The schnapps doesn't want to go down your throat. It just seems to stay suspended somewhere and you can't swallow." He was silent, and then he shrugged. "Well, now I had a thousand crowns for my newspaper, and from the Gestapo, of all places."

"And now you became a complete fool," Holm said.

"That's a matter of opinion, Pastor," the man said.

Peter, peering in the darkness, could see the laughter in the man's eyes. He could tell only from that. The rest of his face was in no condition to show emotion of any kind.

"What this man did next was the act of a consummate idiot," the priest said, but now there was a slight smile around his mouth.

The man accepted a bottle of beer from Lars and drank from the bottle with his good hand.

"Can you say what it was?" Peter asked him, looking now at the bandaged hand.

"Of course," the priest said. "What this idiot did was this. He printed a receipt for the money in the paper."

Peter frowned. Lars burst out into a great laugh. Even Lise giggled.

Peter looked at the other faces. "I don't understand," he said.

"He printed a receipt in the paper," Holm repeated. "A proper, formal receipt. He acknowledged for everyone to see that the Gestapo had donated a thousand crowns, and he thanked the Gestapo and told them it would help double the circulation of his paper."

"And it did, too," the man said.

Peter began to chuckle. The man nodded approvingly and patted him with his bandaged hand, gently.

Holm looked at everyone disapprovingly. "That's

right, laugh with him. You're all fools." But then he couldn't keep his own face serious any longer, and he started to laugh.

"That wasn't all," the priest said. "He also asked— in print, mind you—that in the future the Gestapo not bother to make contact with him personally but to leave any additional contributions at any newspaper kiosk in the city and they would be received gratefully." The priest chuckled for a moment, and then his face became serious. "Very funny, yes, I'll admit that, but what happened afterward was not so funny, was it, my friend?"

The man finished the beer and set the bottle down carefully. "No, as a matter of fact, it was not funny at all."

"You see," Holm said, "they caught up with him again, and this time they didn't walk along the canal and have a drink, but they took him to Gestapo headquarters in Shell House in Copenhagen, and being Germans, they couldn't see any humor in the affair, none at all. They would not have liked him in any circumstances, his having published the things he has, but now they had a special, personal reason for disliking him. He had made fools of them, and they do not like that. And they showed their dislike. Most precisely."

The man touched his face and, despite himself, winced. "It wasn't pleasant," he said. "But it was bearable. The questionings were bad enough. But the worst was the solitary confinement between times. After a few days of that, I thought I would lose my mind."

"Because you had no one to play jokes on," Holm said.

"They had transferred me from Shell House to the prison by then, and they put me in one of the cells below the ground. To lie in the dark for days and not know whether it's day or night. There was only one thing that saved me."

Peter leaned forward tensely. "What was that, sir?"

"Gravel," the man said.

"Gravel?" Peter looked puzzled.

"Gravel," the man repeated. "I was being taken back to my cell one day after a particularly intensive questioning." He glanced at his bandaged hand. "On the way I slipped and fell. I wasn't quite myself, you understand. But as I fell I had an idea, and I'm quite proud of myself, because my head was not exactly in the best condition for ideas at the moment; I grabbed a handful of gravel. When I was thrown back into the cell I counted the gravel. I had exactly eleven pieces. I scattered them in the dark, and then I started searching for them. I used to count, slowly, evenly, until I collected each of the eleven pieces. Then every day I used to try to better my time." He reached into his pocket with his good hand and took out a handful of gravel. "There it is, son. You wouldn't think that lot could keep you sane, would you? I'll keep these little things for the rest of my life."

He slipped the gravel back into his pocket and accepted another bottle of beer from Lars and then he said to Peter, "And now there's just one other thing you want to know about, isn't there?" He held up his bandaged hand. "How I got that?"

Peter nodded. "Yes, sir."

"A little Gestapo speciality, son," the man said. "It's supposed to help loosen your tongue."

"Lars," Lise said.

"He can hear," Lars said quietly.

"They dip a little piece of cotton wool in petrol and

88

put it between your fingers and light it," the man said.

Peter felt his stomach turn.

"It has to be done exactly right," the man said. "The Gestapo takes pride in doing things perfectly, especially their technique of making people talk. There must be exactly the right amount of petrol, just enough to soak the piece of cotton. It must not spread over the skin or else the whole hand catches fire at once, and that ruins the whole idea. It has to be done with great skill so that the flame is only between the fingers. And they start between the little finger and ring finger of the left hand and move across the hand. Then they move to the right hand. And after that, of course, they have all the toes." He shook his head. "What a waste of good petrol."

The man drank the last of the beer and closed his eyes. Even the way the Gestapo had left it, the face could not hide the exhaustion.

"You'd better catch a little sleep," Lars said.

The man took a puff on his cigarette. "Thanks, old man," he said to Lars. "And to you, ma'am." He held out his good hand to Peter. "And thanks for listening to me, lad."

"Oh, I enjoyed it," Peter said quickly. Then his face reddened. "I mean . . ."

"You enjoyed it," the man said. "And you can pay no greater compliment to a writer than to tell him you enjoy his stories."

He stood up and then he swayed and Pastor Holm leaped to his feet to help him, but the man recovered and waved the priest away. He walked slowly to the old divan in the corner of the basement and stretched out. "Young man," he said to Peter.

Peter walked over to the divan. "Yes, sir?"

"Isn't there one more question you want to ask me?"

Peter hesitated. "No, sir."

"Are you certain?"

Peter looked at the man with the battered face and then at his father and then at his mother and the priest. Then he said, "There is one question."

"I knew it," the man said. His voice was very tired, but he smiled.

"How did you get away? From the prison."

The man nodded. "I'm glad you asked the question, lad. You would have been a poor son of a newspaperman not to want to find that out. Well, it's too late to go into it in detail. We'll save that for another time. I'll just tell you that a colonel in the Gestapo went to the prison with a signed order for my release."

"Gosh," Peter said.

"Yes?" the man asked, looking at Peter questioningly.

"Did he want to take you somewhere else?"

"No."

Peter frowned. "Why would a colonel in the Gestapo . . ." Then he broke into a grin, a big grin. "It wasn't a real colonel! It was someone from the Underground, dressed up as a Gestapo colonel . . ."

The man reached out and punched Peter on the arm. He looked at Lars. "Watch out, old man. It won't be too long before you have some real competition here."

With that he turned his face to the wall and was instantly asleep. Pastor Holm settled himself in the chair and stretched out his long legs.

When Peter got up in the morning, the priest and the

90

man were gone. That evening Lars told him Holm had
taken the man to the Tuborg brewery, where he had been
treated by a doctor in the clinic there and then had been
sent from the Tuborg dock over to Sweden.

15

ABOUT TWO WEEKS LATER LARS RETURNED FROM HIS OFFICE IN
Copenhagen with pleasant news. A colleague of his at the
newspaper had offered him the use of his summer hut
on the north coast of Sealand for the weekend. Although
the little cottage was designed primarily for summer use,
it had a big stove in the kitchen and a fireplace in the living room and could be made comfortable in all but the
severest weather.

Lars spoke with enthusiasm, but Peter could not escape the feeling that his father's thoughts were elsewhere.
When Lise asked Lars whether they should take time for a
holiday, even a brief one, Lars replied, "I'm trying to work
out something in my mind. I think a few days on the coast
might be just the ticket."

When Lars said that, in that way, Lise agreed immediately.

Through a friend who managed the taxi office in Elsinore, they engaged a cab. They dressed warmly, took simple food, sleeping bags that had last been used long before
on hunting trips, and set out.

They rode through Elsinore, along the north Sealand

coast, through Hornbaek to Gilleleje, and then followed a smaller road until they reached the cottage. Lars arranged for the taxi to pick them up on Sunday evening.

The summer hut was situated on a grassy slope that lead to a broad, sandy beach. It was a typical summer cottage, but it was well made and snug, and by kind chance the weather was fairly mild at the moment and the winter wind was not too angry and the waters of the open Kattegat lapped peacefully on the shore.

Peter and his father got the stove working in the kitchen and then built a fire in the living room. It was a pleasant house. The kitchen was painted in a cheery blue and white and the living room was paneled in light wood. The place soon was cosy.

Lars suggested a walk along the beach before it got too dark. Lise said she thought she should unpack and get dinner prepared, so Lars and Peter went out by themselves.

The water was the color of steel. With the oncoming evening the wind rose. Here and there on the wide sea they could make out ships, some of them moving, others riding at anchor.

"Do you remember that man who spent a few hours at our house a few weeks ago?" Lars asked.

"The one who had been in prison? The one with the burned hand?"

"Yes. I received a word from him today."

"Did you? Is he back?"

"He's still in Sweden. But he is much better. Even his hand. He sent his thanks and his special regards to you." Lars picked up a long piece of driftwood and using it as a staff, strode along the beach. "He said if we met him we probably wouldn't recognize him. He said he has his own face again, outside of a few missing teeth."

"That was a wonderful thing to do," Peter said. "I mean, whoever dressed up in a Nazi uniform and got him out."

"Yes, it was."

"It was pretty stupid of the Germans, wasn't it?"

"From our point of view. But then the man was in a genuine Gestapo uniform, he spoke perfect German and he had all the proper credentials. The Germans are a very orderly people, and they believe what they hear and see and read."

"How did he get all those things, the uniform and everything?"

"Well, the lads on our side are getting better and better at their trade."

"Do you know the man who pretended?"

"Yes."

"He must be very brave."

"He is very brave. He also has a fine sense of humor. He thought it was a great joke to play on the Germans. Particularly since they don't have a very great sense of humor."

Peter spotted another piece of driftwood and ran over and picked it up. He liked these times, he guessed, better than anything—being with his father, doing what his father was doing. He wondered whether he would grow as tall as his father. He was tall for his age, but his father was very tall.

Of course he loved his mother. There was no question

about anything like that. With his mother, his father and he made the family. And that was something. But this was different, being alone with his father, walking along a beach, just the two of them.

Walking along, smelling the salt air, the sand yielding under his feet, he remembered, for some reason, a time a few summers before, when his father had taken them to visit some relatives in Jutland. He remembered everything about that time—crossing the water in the train on the boat, visiting Odense, crossing more water, and then riding through Jutland.

Jutland was not very far away from where they lived, in miles, not really; people living in ordinary sized countries would not think it was any distance at all. But it was a strange and wonderful adventure for Peter. The people spoke with a funny accent, and in so many places along the coast it was wild and open and the water was violent and the waves rolled high and broke with a roar.

There was a Viking feeling in that part of Denmark. There were many more German soldiers there and there were many places barred for military reasons, but it was still possible to feel the open land and the open sea and the sense of other lands far away. Even though strangers from a foreign country were there to tell them where they could go on their own land and where they could not.

But of all the exciting things that happened on that holiday, for some reason Peter did not yet understand, one small incident remained most vividly in his mind. It was nothing terribly exciting, but he could recall it now, at this moment, walking along the beach. It was a day pouring with rain. It was not cold, but the rain came down

94

in buckets. Even now, with the water slapping lazily on the shore, he could hear that rain, that time.

Lars suddenly had felt like a walk through the nearby forest. Lise begged off, and Peter went with him. In raincoats and boots they walked along a country road, now mired in mud, and as they walked, not talking in the downpour, Peter noticed that his father seemed to be looking for something. He kept looking at the forest and up at the sky and then at the forest again. Then Lars grunted happily, and he grasped Peter's arm and led him off the road into the forest.

The going was rough. They pushed their way through the underbrush; climbed through brambles and shrubs; were torn at by thorns. Lars studied the ground and from time to time looked up at the sky.

For some reason—Peter remembered it to this day— he did not ask his father what he was looking for, but he knew that his father had not wanted just to take an aimless walk in the rain, that he had something definite in mind. But Peter did not ask what it was. There was something thrilling in not knowing why they were there or where they were going or what his father had in his mind.

Then Lars suddenly raised his hand. He gestured cautioningly and the two of them dropped to their knees. They waited silently for several minutes, their collars turned up against the rain, and Peter knew not to speak, not to question. And then Lars pointed upward.

Peter raised his eyes. Through the rain, high in the air, high above the tall trees, he saw a huge bird flying. The bird was carrying something in its mouth. It flew with its long legs stretched out almost in a straight line behind it and Peter could not make out what it had in its mouth because it flew with its head curled between its shoulders.

The bird flew directly to the top of one of the trees and with a great flapping of wings settled down to what Peter could now see was a nest. And as he watched, the rain pouring down his face, he saw the beaks of small birds jutting up from the nest, and now he could make out that what the big bird had carried was a fish.

Over the sound of the rain he heard a kind of thin peeping from the tree top. He looked quickly at his father, his eyes sparkling, and he saw that his father was not looking at the nest but at him, and there was an expression on his father's face that he had never seen before.

After a moment Lars stood up and walked toward the tree. Peter followed.

When they reached the base of the tree, Lars pointed to small animal footprints in the wet earth. Then he looked up toward the nest.

"That was a heron, Peter," Lars said. He spoke in a whisper. "And the nest up there is called a heronry." Then he pointed again to the tiny prints in the earth. "You see, they are quite fresh; they are not yet filled with water."

"What made those?" Peter asked.

"A fox." Lars looked again up at the heronry. "You see, Peter, the parent herons go out day after day, no matter what the weather is, and they find food for their young. They carry it back, as you saw. But once in a while they drop a fish by mistake. And when they do, there is usually a fox under the tree to retrieve it. The fox runs home and feeds its own young with the heron's catch."

"How does the fox know?"

"So it is in nature," Lars said.

The two of them made their way out of the woods, back to the muddy road, back to the house.

When they returned to the summer hut, Peter realized they had hardly spoken a word. His father had walked along, jabbing the stick into the sand, his mind far away. And Peter, remembering the time of the herons and the fox, had been far away as well.

Lise had dinner ready, and now the wind was high and they felt warm and close and safe in the little hut. But Lars was still somewhere else in his mind. From time to time he rubbed his chin and pursed his lips. Lise asked no questions, and Peter took his cue from her.

After dinner Lars filled a large curved pipe which he smoked only on special occasions, occasions when he was trying to think something out, and he asked Peter, as he held a match over the bowl, "Do you remember what that man told us that night?"

"I think I remember almost everything," Peter said.

"Do you remember especially what he said about his little paper?"

"That was funny."

"What was funny?"

"What he put in the paper, about the Gestapoman trying to bribe him. And then . . ."

"What impressed you most about that part of it?" Lars asked, puffing out great clouds of smoke.

"It was funny, putting a receipt right in the paper."

"And what else?"

Now Peter began to realize that his father had a purpose in his questioning.

"Think, Peter," Lars said gently.

Peter wrinkled his brow. "The Germans read it right away," he said tentatively.

"Exactly. And beyond that?"

After a moment Peter shook his head. "I don't know."

"Certainly you know, Peter," Lars said. "You listened to him as we all did."

Again Peter thought. Then he said doubtfully, "They believed it."

Lars slapped his thigh. "Exactly! They believed it. You've hit upon it, Peter."

Peter looked puzzled. "What did I hit upon?"

Lars jabbed the pipe at his son. "First, the Germans read the paper as soon as it comes out, and then, more importantly, they *believe* what they read. They *believe* what we print in our little papers. They laugh and they pretend it's a pack of lies, but down deep they *believe*." He took a deep drag on his pipe and blew out a vast stream of smoke. "And that gives me my idea."

Lise, who had remained silent until now, said drily, "I knew something has been rummaging around in that head of yours. Your idea about what?"

"About Major Heinz Otto Gruber."

"What are you talking about?" Lise sat up straight at the mention of the name of the Gestapo chief.

"A plan. It's scurrying around in my mind."

"Your plan for what?" Lise asked, although by now she knew.

Lars removed the pipe from his mouth. He gazed at Lise for a long time. "Something has to be done about that swine, Lise. We all know that."

98

"And just what is it you intend to do?" Lise asked, and now her voice was quite still.

"I haven't quite worked it out yet," Lars said. "But I have an idea." He puffed on the pipe. The imitation tobacco smelled like burning hay, which it might very well have been. "It could work, Lise," Lars said. "It could just work."

"If you told me," Lise said in the same still voice, "I might be intelligent about it."

"When I have it worked out," Lars said. "I'll let you see it."

Lars would say nothing more. He was, Peter thought, like that English detective, Sherlock Holmes, tall and skinny and puffing on a big curved pipe. And now and then he chuckled to himself, but he would not tell Lise or Peter what it was that amused him.

The next two days were spent quietly, walking, talking, the three of them being close. Apart from the occasional appearance of German soldiers, it might have been an ordinary weekend on the coast, in an ordinary time.

The air seemed freer here. They could see for long distances, and they truly felt alone most of the time and they talked of many things, none of them very important, but all without worry and fear.

The hours went swiftly. Sunday afternoon arrived unexpectedly, unwanted, and too soon. They pitched in and cleaned the place thoroughly, repacked, saw the fires were extinguished, the shades drawn. They were ready when the taxi arrived.

On the way home, oddly enough, as much as he had enjoyed the weekend, Peter found himself recalling the other time in Jutland, and how it was that the fox would be waiting if the fish slipped out of the mouth of the heron.

16

FOR THE NEXT FEW DAYS LARS SAID NOTHING ABOUT HIS scheme, whatever it was. And then he spent an evening in the cellar typing out the stencil for that week's edition of the little paper.

He came upstairs for a cup of coffee, and there was laughter in his eyes, but he still remained silent even though Peter and Lise looked at him questioningly. Coffee in hand, he returned to the basement, and Peter went back to his schoolwork.

It was about ten o'clock when Lars emerged from the basement again. This time he had a copy of the paper run off from the stencil. He read through it with a maddening slowness, pretending not to notice the impatience of his wife and son, and then, with a laugh, he held out the paper.

Both grabbed it and looked at it at the same time. The first thing that caught their eyes was the headline across the top of the page:

A FRIENDLY GESTAPO LEADER

Lise and Peter raised their eyes in astonishment. Lars was grinning from ear to ear. Peter and his mother read on:

It is not very often that this or any other
Occupied country has occasion to say a

kind word about the Gestapo. It is there-
fore particularly pleasant to be able to
pay our compliments to Major Heinz
Otto Gruber, the chief of the Gestapo in
Elsinore.

Again Peter and his mother looked up. "Lars, have
you lost your mind?" she asked.

"Read it, read it," he said.

Unlike most of his colleagues, who appear to delight in brutality, Major Gruber has shown himself to be understanding; one might say even compas-
sionate. His leniency in dealing with the
problems he has to face; his willingness
to give everyone the benefit of the
doubt; his many demonstrations of
mercy; have won him many friends in
the area over which he has jurisdiction.

The Nazi ideal may well be "ruthless
toughness" but we are indeed fortunate
in having to deal with a gentleman who
has not forgotten some of the more decent aspects of life.

It is not the happiest thing to be under
the rule of foreigners. But if it must be
so, then let it be under an officer such
as Major Heinz Otto Gruber.

Lise finished reading the article first. She looked up
stupefied. "Is this some kind of joke?"

Lars nodded joyfully. "You might call it that. You
might very well call it that."

"Are you going mad or am I?" Lise asked.

When Peter, utterely confused, raised his eyes from

the paper Lars grabbed it from him, looked at it, and then began dancing around the room.

"You are mad," Lise said.

"Yes," Lars said. "It's a kind of joke, and if it works, it will be a terrible joke." He held the paper in front of him. "Peter," he said, "don't you understand? Your mother never was very bright, but I've been having high hopes for you."

Peter looked at his mother in bewilderment.

Lars waved the page. "This is a kind of weapon," he said, lowering his voice conspiratorially. "A kind of secret weapon."

"You've been working too hard," Lise said.

"Words, Peter, words, louder than bombs, deadlier than bullets."

"Lars," Lise said. "Why don't you just lie down for a while?"

"Peter, are you thinking?"

"Yes, Father."

"Peter, I'll give you a clue. The man who was here with the bandaged hand. What did we learn from him?"

"That the Germans read his paper."

"And . . . ?" Lars coaxed with his fingers as though they were playing charades. "And, Peter, and . . . ?"

Peter concentrated. "That they believed it . . ."

Lise's eyes widened. "Lars . . ."

Lars nodded, snapping his fingers. "You're getting it. You're both getting it . . ."

"They'll read this," Peter said, excitement edging into his voice.

"And believe it?" Lise asked.

"They'll believe Major Gruber is getting soft," Peter said.

Lars broke into a fresh grin. "They say six months in Denmark makes a weak Nazi, don't they? They invented that themselves, didn't they?"

"But, Lars, they know better here," Lise said.

"Here, yes. Copenhagen, yes, or perhaps just maybe. But Germany? Berlin?" He looked at the little sheet of paper. "It looks so innocent. But it's a time bomb. If it goes off . . ."

Lise began to laugh, the deep laugh that seemed to start in her heart and never get past her throat. "Lars . . . you are clever."

"Clever?" Lars shouted. "Clever? What kind of vocabulary do you possess? Doesn't the word 'brilliant' occur to you? Doesn't 'genius' pass through your mind? I'm always clever, day in and day out. But this . . ." He looked reverently at the sheet of paper. "Words, Peter, words. Remember, the greatest weapon, the greatest weapon of them all."

17

"A STROKE OF GENIUS HAS TO BE MEMORIALIZED," LARS SAID. "Peter . . . ?"

"Yes, Father, I understand what memorialize means."

"No, my boy, you do not."

"It means . . ."

"It means a splendid dinner and then a splendid evening running off our splendid paper with its glowing tribute to our splendid Gestapo chief. That's what it means."

"I'll do the best I can," Lise said, still laughing.

"Not at all," Lars said. "Not one of your splendid dinners. One of the splendid dinners at the inn."

The smile faded from Lise's mouth. "Do you want to go there?"

After a moment Lars said, "It won't be the same, will it, without him. But this little joke of mine, it's the kind of thing Oscar Jensen would have liked. Wherever he may be at this moment, I think he would appreciate our eating in his inn on the day when we may just possibly have arranged the future of his dear and gentle German friend."

They stood just inside the door of the inn and looked around.

"It isn't the same," Lise said. "I don't like it here any more."

"Perhaps it wasn't such a good idea to come here after all," Lars said.

They would have left but at that moment the head waiter, an old friend, rushed up to them.

"Lars," he said. "Lise, I haven't seen you . . ."

"Yes," Lars said.

"And Peter," the man said. "I am happy to see you, all of you. Come with me."

He led them to a table and they sat down. Lars looked around. The inn was crowded at this time of evening. There were two large groups of Germans gathered round two different tables. The Germans, as usual, were talking at the tops of their voices.

Lars listened to them for a moment. "My goodness, what a happy day it will be when our people will be able to eat and drink in our own restaurants without being afraid someone is listening to them. Look around you. Except for the Germans everybody is whispering."

"I thought everybody spoke that way in restaurants," Peter said. "Except for Germans."

Lars contemplated his son. His eyes were suddenly somber. "Did you hear that, Lise? Peter said he thought people always whispered in restaurants, outside of the Germans. Do you realize what that means, Lise? Peter cannot remember when people laughed and spoke naturally and didn't have fear in their hearts." His mouth tightened. "War does many strange things, but I never quite realized how it can pervert the understanding of the young." He put his hand over Peter's. "One day, son, and before too long, I hope and pray you will discover that this is not the normal way for people to have a meal with their friends in a public place. Danes can be quite noisy people, and you will find that out when this filthy business is ended."

The waiter arrived with their drinks. Lars and Lise raised their glasses of aquavit and said "Skol." They held each other's eyes as they drank and then in the Danish manner tilted the empty glasses to each other.

"I cannot wait for that day," Lars said, setting down his glass.

"Is that true?" Lise asked.

"Is what true?"

"That you cannot wait for the war to end?"

"My goodness, what a funny question that is."

"I wonder if it is true, down deep in your heart."

"Of course it's true. How can you doubt that?"

After a moment she smiled and said, "All right."

"What did you mean?" Lars asked.

"Nothing."

"I want to know."

She was silent again for a moment. Then she said, "I think, with everything that is happening, you are enjoying yourself, Lars."

"Enjoying myself? I never thought of it that way."

"The danger, the excitement. Life will seem pretty dull when this is all over."

Lars filled their glasses again. "I'll settle for that dullness, Lise, starting right now."

"I hope so," she said.

He looked at her across the table. "This has been on your mind."

She nodded, smiling. "Yes, it has. I often wonder what the hours and the days will be able to offer you when all these unpleasant people go. Just to go to work at your regular newspaper, write ordinary, unexciting, normal stories, drive back and forth in an ordinary car, using petrol instead of puffing along like a burning barn. No picking up secret messages and dropping off other equally secret messages. No more of that constant, tingling, wondering if you're going to get caught." She turned her eyes from Lars to Peter. "It's even got into his blood now," she said quietly. "How will he adjust to life as an ordinary Danish schoolboy when the war is over?"

Lars looked at her soberly and then burst into a loud laugh. It made a large sound in the room.

"I will answer you, my precious little Lise. I will answer you," he said. "No one who is married to you need fear boredom. You're enough mystery and secret messages, and I've often had that tingling feeling, wondering whether I'd be caught." He stopped with great abruptness. "Can't talk about that in front of the boy," he said gruffly.

Lise grinned. Whatever she was going to say she did not say, because the room suddenly filled with the sound of singing. The German soldiers at one of the tables, filled with Danish food and Danish snaps and Danish beer, had begun a sentimental journey.

"That's exactly what we needed," Lars said.

"It's nice to think they'll be happy to go home," Lise said.

Lars pursed his lips. "I don't know. I have been to Germany. I prefer Denmark."

"That's because you're a Dane," Peter said.

Lars considered that soberly. "Our son is sprouting into a philosopher, Lise. Tell me, philosopher, how do you feel about the war ending?"

"That depends who wins," Peter said.

"That is not open for discussion," Lars said.

"You mean when the Germans lose and go home?"

"Hopefully, with their tails between their legs."

Peter shrugged. "I guess it will be all right."

"All right?" Lars echoed softly. "Did you hear that, Lise? He guesses it will be all right." The singing grew louder. Lars gazed across the room for a moment. "All right, the boy says. Is that the new generation? The department of understatement? The old British stiff upper lip? All right? Is that the best you can come up with?"

"Lars, stop teasing him," Lise said.

"No, I want to know. All right? Does that have a significance for the younger generation that escapes one of my advanced age?"

The waiter arrived with the first course.

When he left, Lars asked, "All right?"

"I don't know," Peter said. "I can't remember much how it was before the war. I guess I'll like it better, but I don't know."

"You probably won't like it better at all," Lise said.

"Lise," Lars said.

"It's true," she said. "It's true of him as it's true of you. You'll remember these days and all the dangerous games we've played. That's what always makes the next war. The memory plays tricks. Only the exciting things, the funny things; only they are remembered. The cruelties, the deaths—one forgets about them."

"My goodness," Lars said mildly. "We are getting so serious." He started eating, and then the laugh sprang back to his face. "I have something funny to tell both of you." He ate another mouthful. "Lise, you know something? Wouldn't it be wonderful if once in a while, say once a month, we could publish a proper paper? I mean with proper type. Then we would be able to print photographs as well."

"We have enough problems now," she said. "What is the funny thing you want to tell us?"

"That's what made me think about it. You see, about three weeks ago some RAF men had to make a forced landing here. They were taken in hand by one of the groups. One of the men was burned, rather badly. They gave him a good Danish name and shoved him into a hospital. He's still there, but he'll be all right."

"Why is that funny?" Peter asked.

108

"I'm coming to the funny part," Lars said. "The two other RAF men were taken to Copenhagen and hidden there. Then they were told one day that arrangements had been made to smuggle them over to Sweden. One of them said what a shame it was that he hadn't got to see Copenhagen. He said he had so often wanted to visit our little city and there he was in the middle of it and he was going to be whisked away without having had a single look.

"Well, my goodness, that was too much, of course. Our boys couldn't disappoint him that way. The RAF men were already in ordinary civilian clothes by now, so they just took them out for a tour of the city. One of the places they visited was a large cafe, and there were German officers there of course, and one of the RAF men happened to take out a cigarette." He looked at Peter and held up his hand. "Don't worry, they were Danish cigarettes. The Underground boys thought of that. Anyway, one of the German officers immediately whipped out a lighter, very gallant and polite he was, and he offered a light to the RAF man. Such an expression of chivalry between enemies! Only the German couldn't quite appreciate that, could he?

"Well, you know, there is a girl who goes around taking pictures. The Germans are very sentimental, and they love to have pictures taken. She caught the immortal moment. The German officer was quite proud. He thought it was marvelous evidence of the good feeling between Germans and Danes."

Lars ate some more food and drank some aquavit. He poured Lise and himself another drink and then pretended he had just noticed Peter, who was leaning forward, his mouth open. "Close that mouth, Peter," Lars said. "My goodness, are you catching flies?"

"That isn't the end of the story, is it, Father?"

"It certainly will be if you don't eat some food," Lise said.

"No," Lars said, "that is not the end of the story. The best part is coming. You see, one of our boys got hold of that picture and sent it over to Sweden, along with the RAF men. And the next day one of the papers in Sweden published the picture on the front page—the German officer with a silly smile on his face offering a light to a man who appeared to be an ordinary Danish citizen. But the caption under the picture was this: 'In a Copenhagen cafe a German officer extends a courtesy to an officer of the Royal Air Force. Another RAF flier watches. It must be added that both British fliers are back in England to fly again.' "

By now Lise was giving that throaty laugh and Peter was laughing out loud.

"But you see," Lars said. "The really funny thing would be if I could put that picture in a paper here. Can you imagine that?" He shook his head, chuckling.

A German soldier, listing on his way to the bar, paused at the table. He listened to the laughter, swaying slightly. "You are happy, you are all happy," he said in fair Danish.

The Andersens stopped their laughter.

"Yes," Lars said. "We are very happy."

"That is your wife?"

"Yes," Lars said.

"And your son?"

110

"Yes."

The German looked from one to the other in drunken concentration. "It is a good family," he pronounced. "No wonder you are happy." He straightened, clicked his heels, and for some reason found it necessary to salute. He lurched off toward the bar.

"There you have it," Lars said. "The ultimate commendation. We have been rated as a good family by the conqueror."

The good feeling was gone, and Lise tried to recapture it. "You agree, don't you?" she asked, trying for her smile.

"I don't know," Lars said. "I always thought so, but now I don't know."

The fun seemed gone for the moment. Lars paid the bill and they started out of the inn. They were met at the door by the head waiter.

"Was everything all right?" he asked.

"It was fine," Lars said.

"Did you enjoy your dinner?"

"Yes," Lise said. "Yes, thank you."

The head waiter nodded. "But it is not the same."

"No," Lars said. "It is not the same."

He started to go but the waiter took his arm. "Lars, don't let so much time pass before you come again."

"No," Lars said.

"It is not the same," the man said. "But we cannot allow it to become so much not the same."

Lars nodded. They left the inn. The night had become very cold, and the air smelled of the sea. Lars started to chuckle again. Lise looked up happily. The food had been good and the drinks had been good and she was feeling well again after her illness and she was delighted that Lars had regained his humor.

"You know," Lars said. "When they told me about the RAF men, they told me something else. I must put it in next week's paper. There is a clothing factory here in Sea-land, and now it has to make uniforms for German soldiers. Well, if you can imagine this, some of the Underground lads got in there the other night, and do you know what they did? They squirted itching powder into the uniforms." He started to shake with laughter.

"Is that really true?" Peter asked.

"Of course it's true," Lise giggled. She held tightly to Lars' arm, grateful that the German soldier hadn't spoiled the evening. "Everything your father says is always true."

"My goodness," Lars said. "Can you imagine that sight? The whole company lined up. And the Germans sweat. You know how much Germans sweat."

"Lars," Lise said.

"Only it would have to be a moving picture camera for that. All of them jumping up and down scratching themselves."

"Lars," she said again.

He knew her voice well—all its sounds. He knew her voice and its message even when it was mixed with laughter, half the laughter still there, half of it already gone. He looked ahead and saw the black car and turned swiftly and saw the other end of the street was decorated the same way.

"Just drop back," he said.

"No," Lise said.

"It may be nothing," Lars said. "It may have nothing to do with me."

"Yes," she said.

A wild thought flashed through Peter's mind: they might be looking for him.

"Until we know what it is," Lars said to Lise. "Just drop back."

"I will not."

"Peter."

"Yes, Father." His heart was racing again, and he felt that thing in his stomach.

"Take your mother's hand."

"Lars, I will not leave you," Lise said. "Peter, you go away."

"Peter," Lars said. He said the name almost in a whisper.

Peter took his mother's hand. She tried to pull away, but she was quite small, and he was a strong boy and he held her.

"Now just drop back," Lars said.

"Lars," she said.

She tried to pull away from Peter, but he held her tightly. They watched Lars walk ahead, and Peter thought his father had straightened up somehow and had got taller because his hands stuck so far out of his coat sleeves and his trousers seemed too short.

"Oh, God!" Lise said, and now she did not try to pull away from Peter. She twisted her hand so that she was holding his wrist as well.

They watched Lars move farther and farther ahead of them. Now he slipped his hands into his pockets against the cold and he hunched his shoulders and he walked almost jauntily as though the last thing he had on his mind was an encounter with the Gestapo.

Lise and Peter watched slowly and her fingers dug into his wrist. They saw three men in dark coats and dark hats step out of the shadows, and the three men blocked Lars' way. Lise and Peter stood still and held each other and watched.

"Oh, God," Lise said again. She lurched forward. "Let me go!"

"He said to stay back," Peter said. He was glad he had something to do, something his father had told him to do, because he knew if he hadn't this responsibility he might do something childish. He was too old for tears. Boys almost twelve don't cry, but he was glad he had a job to do so he never would find out whether he was too old or not.

Lise pulled hard. "Let me go," she said fiercely.

Peter held her. His mother was very strong now, but he was stronger.

"Oh, my God," Lise said. "Oh, my God."

The three men in the dark coats and dark hats had finished talking to Lars now, and they led him to the black car and Lars climbed in and for one moment when he was getting into the car, he glanced back at his wife and his son, and then he was inside and the men had followed him in and the doors were slammed shut and the car went off.

"Oh, my God," Lise said.

Now Peter let her go. They both stared up the street. It was empty. The night air was brilliant and clear, and it was as though nothing had happened.

114

"God in heaven," Lise said in a voice so low it was hardly said.

Peter bit his lips. He wished he had something else to do, because he was beginning to feel that perhaps boys almost twelve might not be too old for that after all.

Then he remembered something. "Mother," he said. When Lise, still staring at the empty street did not answer, he said, "Mother, listen to me."

"They've arrested your father, Peter," she said.

"Mother, listen. The machine."

"It was as though I saw it all before, as though I'd seen everything that happened."

He took her hand. "Listen to me, Mother. We have to get everything out of the house. The machine, the paper, the pads and ink and stencils. We've got to get them out of the house."

When she still did not answer, he took her hand and led her down the street. She walked with him as though she were a child.

18

"WE'LL MAKE TWO PACKS OF IT," PETER SAID. "IT'LL BE easier to carry."

"Yes," Lise said. Her voice was flat and empty.

Peter stole a quick look at his mother. Since they had returned home that was the only word she had said— "Yes"—to whatever he had suggested, and he knew she was not hearing him at all. "What do you think we can wrap this up in?" he asked. He had made one neat pile of the paper, ink, and other things. The machine itself, he decided, would be wrapped separately.

"Yes," Lise said.

"Mother!"

She looked at him and smiled. "Yes, Peter?"

"What can we wrap this up in? So that it won't attract too much attention."

"Yes," she said again, but this time she said it in a different way. She breathed in deeply. "Let me see," she said, looking around. Then she turned swiftly to Peter and put her arms around him. "Peter . . ."

"I know, Mother, but we have to get rid of all this. They may come here."

She nodded rapidly and straightened. She looked around again. Her eyes were dead but dry. "A couple of blankets," she said.

"Good," Peter said, because it was a good idea and because his mother seemed to be pulling herself together. "Blankets are just right. And we might be able to use them to keep warm later on."

"Later on? Where? Why?"

"The Boy Scouts say 'Be Prepared.' " He shrugged. "Who knows?"

"We're coming back here, Peter," Lise said.

"Sure."

"We're coming back to our house."

"Yes."

"We're coming back and your father is coming back, and all these things we're taking out of the house, they're coming back too, Peter."

116

"Yes, Mother. But let's hurry now."

"These are your father's tools, the tools of his trade. He'll want them when they release him."

"Then we'll bring them back," Peter said. "I'll get the blankets."

He ran upstairs and took two blankets from the beds and ran back down to the cellar. His mother was standing as he had left her, stiffly, her arms crossed over her breast.

He put the mimeograph machine into one of the blankets and wrapped the blanket around it securely. He folded it so he could sling it over his shoulder. Then he wrapped the other things in the second blanket.

"We'd better go right now, Mother," he said.

"Where will we go, Peter?"

"Gosh, I never thought about that. Where can we go?"

She put her arm around him and smiled. It was a pale, tired smile. "I'm all right, Peter. It was unnerving, a little unnerving, but I'm all right, and I know exactly where to go. You see, your father thought this might happen one day, it almost had to happen, and he told me what to do. Pastor Holm. He told me if we ever needed help to go to the priest. That he would know what to do. He said if anything ever happened to him, go to Pastor Holm and now something has happened, and that's where we must go." She drew away and shivered for a moment and crossed her arms again.

They went upstairs, each of them carrying one of the bundles, and they put on their hats and coats. Lise looked around.

"I don't know why I'm doing this," she said. "We'll

be back again very soon, perhaps even tonight."

At the door she looked back. "I'm so silly," she said angrily. "Your father would laugh at me."

It was late now and colder, and they were both aware of what they were carrying and they were both terrifyingly aware that Lars was not with them, and not that he was just away somewhere, but that he was away in a special way, with the German Gestapo, with the Nazi secret police.

They trudged slowly, bending now and again against the night wind, taking back roads and narrow country lanes, and the snow crunched under their feet and the air was razor sharp—not just the wind but the air itself— and the sky was clear. It was dark, very dark.

It was cold and dark and quiet and deserted—an empty, abandoned winter world—and the only sounds were the sounds of their footsteps and their breathing. Their thoughts were silent.

19

PASTOR HOLM WAS NOT SURPRISED TO SEE THEM. HE STOOD outside the door of the rectory and gestured for them to go in. He glanced around swiftly and followed them, closing the door and bolting it.

"Lars," Lise said, breathing a little hard, from the walk and the bundle, and what was going on inside her.

"I know," the priest said.

"You know? You know already?" Peter asked in surprise. "It just happened, a couple of hours ago."

"Yes," Pastor Holm said.

"Then perhaps you know more," Lise said. "What's happening to him? Will they release him? Perhaps they've already let him go."

"Sit down, Lise," the pastor said.

Lise's eyes opened wider. "That's bad," she said, the stillness coming back into her voice. "When you tell me to sit down it's bad. I can hear it standing. What is it, Palle?" She stopped and then she asked, "He isn't . . . ? Palle, they haven't . . . ?"

Holm took her hand and shook his head gently. "No, Lise, he is not dead."

"Then that's all right," Lise said. "Do you have a cigarette, Palle? Then he's all right. They just want to ask him a few questions. He'll know how to answer them." She took a cigarette from Holm and leaned forward as he held out a light. "He's cleverer than that lot. Especially Major Gruber." She dragged on the cigarette and sat down. "They'll probably let him go before morning. That Gruber is an idiot."

"Lars is no longer at Elsinore," Holm said.

She looked up at him.

"They've taken him to Copenhagen, to Vestre prison."

She sat there for a moment, the cigarette burning between her fingers. "Is that bad, Palle?"

"I don't know. It's not bad and it's not good. They just took him there."

"But it could be bad," she said.

"Lise, let's not jump to conclusions. Certainly it could be bad. Anything connected with the Gestapo can be bad. How bad it is, I don't know. They may just be picking up

119

people for the record, so they can show Berlin how active and efficient they are. It might be nothing more than that."

Lise nodded. "You're right, Palle. It probably is the Gestapo just showing it's the Gestapo." She drew deeply on the cigarette and then seemed to have trouble getting the smoke out of her. But she went on quickly, "They'll probably release him after they finish asking him a few silly questions. Even if they find out about the little paper. After all, Palle, even if they know about that, even if they know Lars writes it and publishes it, that's not such a serious crime, a little paper . . ." She stopped.

She stared at Pastor Holm for several moments, and to Peter, whose eyes were on her, her face seemed to grow old, like a trick of makeup, like something on a film screen. It got old and very, very tired.

"It is not just our little paper, is it, Palle?" she asked.

"No, Lise."

She nodded, the way an old woman nods. "Other things, bigger things . . . ?"

"Yes, Lise," the priest said.

"More serious things."

"I cannot lie to you, Lise," Holm said.

"Things that he kept from me, all this time?" she asked.

"He was required to keep them from you, Lise. And it's much better that you do not know."

"That's why Vestre prison. It's too important for Elsinore."

"I presume so," Holm said. He took her hand. "Lise, I'm not trying to minimize this in any way, but we must not assume the worst. We don't know whether this is just another fishing expedition on the part of the Gestapo or whether they know something. Something definite. And if they know something and want to know more, Lars is a strong man. He's strong in every way, inside and out, and he's clever; and they're not the brightest men in the world, those German policemen, even though they would like us to think they are. So we'll just leave it in the hands of God and Lars Andersen. We have good odds, Lise."

After a while Lise saw that the cigarette had burned almost to her fingers, and she had puffed on it only twice. She put the cigarette out slowly. "What do we do, Palle?"

"Wait."

"That other one, the one you brought to our house, the one with the burned hand, you did something about him. You didn't just wait. You got him out."

"If it becomes necessary, something will be done for Lars."

"Necessary." Lise groped around for another cigarette. "And who decides at what moment it becomes necessary?"

He held out the light. "You just must have trust, Lise."

She gestured toward the two blanketed bundles. "What about those?"

"You are required to leave them in my care," Holm said.

"Required, Palle?" she asked. "Required by whom?"

Holm straightened and walked back and forth across the small room. "Lise," he said. "You must understand now that Lars was not working alone and that the little paper was only one of the illegal activities he was involved in. It was the most important thing to him, the little paper, but there were other things which will seem more important to the Germans, and in those things he was not working alone." He paused and looked down at her intently. "He was part of an organization, Lise. You might almost call it a kind of small army, even if they don't wear uniforms. And the only way an army, any army, can function, is by discipline. I am instructed to do something, and when necessary I instruct you to do something and you do it, because Lars was part of this apparatus and by extension, so are you."

"*Was* part of the apparatus, Palle?" Lise asked.

"I'm sorry. Is part of the apparatus."

"Why did you say 'was,' Palle?"

Again the priest took her hand. "Lise, I am not hiding anything from you, I promise you."

She nodded. "All right, Palle, we will leave our things with you, and we will do as you say. We will return home and wait."

"You cannot go home," Holm said.

Lise looked at him. "It's very serious, isn't it, Palle? It's more serious than you are admitting."

"I have told you: anything to do with the Gestapo is serious," Holm said. "Whatever it is, it will not help if the Germans decide to arrest you and Peter and put questions to you too."

"He's right, Mother," Peter said suddenly. Then he looked at the priest abashed.

"Thank you, Peter," Holm said.

"I didn't mean . . ."

"You have a right to express yourself, Peter," Holm said. "You have earned that right."

"You know about Peter?" Lise asked. "You know about him helping?"

"I know quite a bit about Peter," Holm said. The

priest glanced at Peter, and while he did not actually wink at him, it was as though he had.

"Where do we go, Palle?" Lise said. "Where are we required to go?"

"For the moment you remain here," the pastor said.

"For how long?" Lise asked.

Pastor Holm shook his head. "I cannot say."

20

THERE WAS NO NEWS THE NEXT DAY NOR THE DAY after that. And after that the hours went by quietly enough, and Lise learned not to ask questions and after a while not even to look at the pastor as though she expected to hear something.

Holm and his wife, Gudrun, put Lise in a spare room in the upper part of the building, and a bed was set up for Peter in the basement near the furnace.

Each day Holm went about his various duties, some of them quite in keeping with his vocation, so innocent and above board he could have had with him the most fanatical observer from the Gestapo and come off with a clean bill. Other duties were perhaps not so spiritual, at least not from the Nazi point of view.

One afternoon the priest returned home from a visit to an ailing parishioner. It was a bitter day, and the priest's cheeks were red as ripe apples. Warming his hands over the stove, Holm said to Peter, in a conversational manner, "It's too bad you didn't bring your school books here."

"Yes," Peter agreed gravely. "It's too bad."

"You must miss your school and homework."

"Very much," Peter said, falling into the joke.

"It's too bad the Germans are keeping an eye on your house. You could run over there and pick up a few books so you wouldn't fall so much behind."

"Are they?" Peter asked. "Are the Germans really watching our house?"

"From time to time," Holm said.

That was strange news for Peter. His house, that little house, had always seemed so ordinary to him, even when he discovered an illegal paper was being run off in the basement. But to think that now it was being watched.

"Under surveillance," Peter said.

"I beg your pardon?"

"That's the official phrase. Under surveillance."

"It is indeed," Holm said. "That's quite a word. Surveillance."

"From the French. To watch over."

"Is that so? I didn't know you were studying French."

"I'm not. My father told me that. It was one of the words I didn't know."

"I don't understand."

"It's something that happens with us," Peter said. "A kind of game. My father likes to use big words sometimes, not big words, really, but different words, words other people don't always use, and he always asks me if I know what they mean, and usually I do, or I think I do, but sometimes I don't at all, and 'surveillance' was one of those I didn't know."

Holm nodded gravely. "Yes, surveillance is an excellent word and wholly appropriate. Well, Peter, your house is under Gestapo surveillance."

Peter grinned. "I wonder what the neighbors are thinking."

"It must not be very hard for them to figure out what has happened."

"It's funny, in a way, your knowing all about all this."

"What's funny about it, Peter?"

"I don't know, Pastor. I was surprised when I found out that my mother and father were getting out an Underground paper, because I never thought of them that way at all."

"How did you think of them?"

"I don't know. My father? He's funny. He can always make me laugh and he can make my mother laugh, and he sees things in a funny way; and when he explains it to me, I can see it in that same funny way."

"But not before that? Not before he explains it to you?"

"Usually not. But anyway, that's the way I thought of him, to make me laugh and to make my mother laugh and take walks and listen to. He seems to know everything without having to look into a book. But I never thought of him doing something secret. Like a book I once read, an English book, about someone called the Scarlet Pimpernel. Everyone thought he was a kind of sissy or something, and all the time he was doing the most exciting things. Nobody ever thought about my father as being any kind of sissy, but I don't think anybody would take him for a secret agent. That's what he is, isn't he, Pastor, a kind of secret agent?"

"You might describe him as such, Peter."

"Pastor Holm, what is happening with my father?"

The priest took his time filling an old, charred, black pipe. "I don't know, Peter."

"Will I see him again?" the boy asked.

The priest held a big wooden match over the pipe bowl. "I hope so, Peter."

"Do you believe so?"

The priest nodded slowly. "I believe so."

"May I ask you something, sir?"

"Certainly."

"How does it feel to you? I mean being mixed up in these things?"

"It feels very good, Peter."

The boy walked to the window and looked across the winter fields.

"Why did you ask that, Peter?" Pastor Holm asked.

Without turning, the boy said. "I don't know. It seems funny for a pastor."

"Funny?"

"It doesn't seem religious. I never thought of you that way. You either."

The priest sat down and puffed several times on his pipe. "It depends how you define religion, doesn't it, Peter?" he asked. "How do you define it?"

Peter turned. "I don't know. Church, I suppose. The words you say."

"The words I say," Holm repeated. He considered for a moment. "The teachings of Jesus Christ make up my religion, true. But Denmark, and what Denmark stands for—that's a part of my religion as well. And freedom is my religion, and decency and justice and love of my fellow man.

And fighting evil, not only the evil of the spirit, but the evil that is on our land—the blight, the disease and anger of one man's tormented mind. I think what I am helping to do is quite religious, come to think of it."

Presently Peter said, "Do you really think I'll see my father again?"

"I believe that, Peter," Pastor Holm said. "I believe it with all my heart."

On the fourth day after Lars Andersen had been picked up by the Gestapo, Lise finally asked the same question.

"What have you heard about Lars?" she asked. "When will they release him?"

"I have heard nothing, Lise," Holm said. "All we know is that he is still in Vestre prison."

"That's all you know." Her face tightened. "Is that supposed to give me some kind of consolation? Is that some kind of triumph, that he is still in Vestre prison?"

"In a way it is," he said. "It would be worse if they were to take him to Germany."

She gazed at him for several moments. The word had dropped like a piece of lead. "Germany?"

"Has my father told them anything?" Peter asked.

"As far as we can find out, no," Holm said.

"I knew that," Peter said. "I knew he wouldn't give them anything."

"How much longer will this go on, Palle?" Lise asked.

"I don't know."

"What is being done for him?"

"I don't know that either."

"What do you know, Palle?" Lise cried. "What do you know?"

"Lise, I know only what I'm told, nothing more," the priest said quietly.

At that moment Gudrun, the pastor's wife, entered the room. "Palle."

The pastor looked up and saw what was on her face. "Where?"

"A black car, Palle, one of the big ones. It is coming toward the house."

Lise's face blanched. Peter went over to her quickly and took her hand.

"I receive visitors from the Gestapo all the time," Pastor Holm said. "They question me and then they leave. All in the line of being good neighbors. Now the two of you go down to the basement and keep quiet, and I'll get rid of our friend, whoever he is. They are quite easy to get rid of. They all want to seem such gentlemen. Now hurry. Be quiet."

Pastor Holm was crouched over his desk working on his Sunday sermon when Gudrun tapped on the door and announced that Major Gruber was there to see him. The pastor removed his glasses and stood up as the Gestapo officer entered the room.

"Major Gruber," he said heartily. "I am glad to see you."

Gruber pulled off his gloves. "Are you?"

The pastor looked around for his pipe. "You know, Major, after some twenty-five years of serving my little flock, the thing I find the biggest nuisance is preparing sermons." He shoved the tobacco into the bowl with his big finger. "Twenty-five years, heavens, can you imagine how many sermons I have delivered? And sometimes I wonder what good they have done."

"Yes," Major Gruber said politely. "May I sit down?"

"Of course, of course. Would you like a cup of coffee?"

"Thank you."

"When I use the word 'coffee,' I am stretching the truth a little, you understand," Holm said. He went to the door and called out to Gudrun. He turned back to the German. "I don't know exactly what it is we use for coffee these days, but perhaps it makes it taste a little better if we do stretch the truth a little."

"Are you concerned about that, Pastor?"

"I'm afraid so, Major," Holm said, lighting his pipe. "I know that one, especially one in my position, should not place too much value on the material things of life, but I do love my coffee."

"I was not referring to coffee, Pastor," Gruber said.

"I beg your pardon?"

"I was referring to truth. Does that concern you?"

"Of course, Major. It's practically my business."

"Good, I am happy to hear that." He took out a cigar. "Will this bother you?"

"Not at all." Holm sat down heavily. He glanced at the pages on his desk and pushed them aside.

"Are you tired, Pastor?" Gruber asked.

"Yes, Major, it has been a long time. I shall be happy when I retire."

"Your parishioners will regret that, I am sure," Gruber said. "It is my understanding that you are very popular with them."

Holm nodded. "Yes, Major, I suppose I am. I always bury their mothers-in-law so they quite disappear."

Gruber laughed jovially. Gudrun entered with a tray. She placed it on a small table, nodded politely to Major Gruber, left the room silently.

The priest poured the coffee. Gruber took the little cup and saucer in his large, red hands and sat back. "You work hard, Pastor."

"These are troubled times," Holm said, pouring his own cup. "My parishioners seem to need me."

"I am sure that's true," Gruber said, sipping the coffee. "In more ways than one."

Holm sipped his own coffee. "In many more ways than one."

"Ways that are not perhaps consistent with your vows," Gruber said.

Holm raised an agreeing hand. "One never can see the future," he said. "Man proposes, God disposes."

Gruber put down the coffee cup and puffed on his cigar, his small, blue eyes looking keenly at the priest. "May I offer you a cigar, Pastor?"

"Thank you, no. I have never acquired a taste for them. Now my wife, Gudrun, she likes one now and then."

The German extracted another cigar from his case and put it on the table. "As a present."

"She will be grateful."

"Pastor Holm," Gruber said. "One or two small things. You get around a great deal. You hear things."

"I do indeed," Holm said, relighting his pipe. "Things you would never believe."

"I would believe, Pastor," Gruber said. "You have

heard about that factory that was blown up the night before last."

"I did," Holm said.

"It was manufacturing military boots for us."

"It seems to me I heard something about that."

"What do you know about it, Pastor?"

Holm shrugged. "Know? Only that this little place was destroyed by explosives."

Gruber broke the ash from his cigar. "Set by whom?"

"I beg your pardon?"

"By whom, Pastor?" Gruber asked quietly.

"I'm sure I don't know, Major."

Gruber drew slowly on the cigar. "You spoke of truth before, Pastor. You're a man of God. You must not lie."

Holm stood up and walked to the same window Peter had stood before a little earlier. He gazed at the snow-covered fields, at the shining trees bending slightly in the wind.

"Did you hear me, Pastor?" Gruber asked in the same quiet voice. "You are a priest. You must not lie."

Still looking at the broad expanse of country he had looked at for many years and loved so well, Pastor Holm said, "Truth is love, Major. And love is truth. If you say something that will hurt someone, then you are telling a lie."

"I am not here to philosophize with you, Pastor," Gruber said. His voice was still quiet but a trace of impatience had entered into it. "I ask you again, what do you know about this latest act of sabotage?"

Holm turned and looked Gruber directly in the face. "Nothing."

"This is a small part of a small country, Pastor," Gruber said. "I daresay almost nothing happens that you do not hear about. I mean hear about all the details. Pastor, we are a civilized people, you know that."

Civilized, the priest thought. It was the word the Germans so loved to use, and always when they were involved in some savagery.

"Yes," he said. "I know that you are considered a civilized country."

"But we cannot continue to tolerate these acts of sabotage," Gruber said. "I think it may just be possible for you to get word to those who are responsible."

"I?"

Gruber blew out a great mouthful of smoke. He smiled. "Look, Pastor, we are both men of the world. I don't want to say foolish and threatening things, not to anyone, least of all to you. But we must all work together. We must cooperate to put an end to these acts of destruction. They can only bring about reprisals. You can understand that. We are fighting a war, Pastor, your war as well as ours. And we must not be hampered in the smallest manner. You do understand, don't you?"

"I understand what you are saying," Holm said.

Gruber's smile widened. "I won't probe too deeply, Pastor, not with you. But you will pass along the word, for the benefit of those involved?"

After a moment Holm said, "If I am able to do so, I will."

"Good." Gruber mashed his cigar into the tray. "I will not keep you. I know how important your wise words will be to your parishioners. You must get on with your sermon. Thank you for the coffee."

"It is my pleasure, Major."

Gruber stood up. He buttoned his greatcoat, which he had not removed, and he began to draw on his gloves. "By the by, Pastor, what has become of Mrs. Lars Andersen and her son?"

"I don't know," Holm said. "I have wondered about that myself."

Gruber fixed his eyes casually on the priest. "We have looked for her everywhere. She seems to have just disappeared." He shrugged. "Ah, well, when she turns up she can make arrangements to have it removed." He picked up his black hat and started for the door. "Good day, Pastor."

"Major Gruber," Holm said.

"Don't bother, Pastor. I can let myself out. Back to the holy words." He raised a hand in farewell.

"Major Gruber," Holm said again.

The Gestapo officer paused at the door. "Yes, Pastor?"

"Major Gruber, have what removed?"

"The body. The body of Lars Andersen." Gruber shook his head. "He had an ailment. It appears no one knew anything about it. A weak heart, I believe it was." He hunched his shoulders. "In any case, it proved fatal. Unfortunate. And we did not know where Mrs. Andersen was, where to bury the body, so we just put it in the prison graveyard. Only for the time being, of course. If you ever manage to locate her, tell her we sympathize with her, and we will cooperate in every way to remove the body to a place of her choosing. Just ask her to come and see me."

He raised his hand in a second farewell.

"Major Gruber," Holm said.

133

"Yes, Pastor?"

"Lars Andersen was one of my parishioners."

"So I have been given to understand. That is why I mention this to you."

"He will be buried in the graveyard next to this church."

"Here, Pastor?" Gruber pursed his lips. "Unfortunately I have no authority to order the body transferred without the specific request of the next of kin." He smiled again. "Get word to the widow, Pastor."

Holm straightened. "Major Gruber," he said harshly. "You have all the authority you need for anything. You had the authority of being responsible for the death of a Dane who was guilty of nothing more than being a patriot."

"I did not kill him, Pastor," Gruber said in a mild voice. "I have already explained to you that his heart was not strong."

"Lars Andersen had nothing wrong with his heart," Palle Holm said. "His heart was filled with love of his country and his countrymen, and it was large enough and strong enough to include Germans who seemed to him to be human beings. When Lars Andersen's heart stopped beating, it was because it had taken more than a strong man can take."

Gruber opened his mouth to say something. He looked at the tall, massive pastor whose face and voice had taken on something new. He closed his mouth without speaking.

"About his earthly remains," Holm said. "I request that you remove him from where he is and bring him here so that I may give my old friend a Christian burial."

134

"I have already explained the impossibility of doing that, under the circumstances," Gruber said.

"Major," Holm said angrily. "Do not take me for a fool. You are playing a game, to draw the widow with the body. Have the grace to be honest about that. But I promise you this, Major, Mrs. Andersen will not appear, and she will not deliver herself into your hands."

Gruber took out his cigar case and inspected the contents. "Then you do know where she is hiding?"

"I asked you not to take me for a fool, Major," Holm said. "And I say only that you will not in any case find her. Now if you have the smallest degree of this civilization you speak so much of, if you possess a drop of Christian charity, you will order the body sent here."

Gruber took out a small silver cigar cutter and nipped the end of his cigar. He broke into an unexpected, sunny smile. "Of course, Pastor, we will send you the body. We are not an unreasonable people. Whatever illegalities Lars Andersen committed, he did so under the illusion that he was being a good Dane. And we Germans understand love of country, even when that love is mistakenly directed a- gainst us. The body will be transferred."

"One thing more, Major," Holm said.

"Yes, Pastor?"

"Do not put spies on my church. Lise Andersen will not be here to attend the services for her husband."

Gruber smiled the bright smile again. "You are in the wrong trade, Pastor," he said. "Of course I will not send observers here. I knew you would have foreseen that."

When the door closed behind the German, the pastor remained motionless, his hands clasped, his head bowed. And through his mind passed unspoken words to commit the soul of Lars Andersen to the keeping of the Lord he did not often commune with, but Whose grace had in many ways guided his life.

When he moved it was with the stiffness of an old man. He made his way to the door to the cellar. "Lise," he said. "Peter."

When they were back in the study, Holm said, "I have something to tell you."

Lise nodded, unsurprised. "Lars."

"Sit down, Lise," Holm said.

" 'Sit down.' There it is again. Then he's dead."

Peter took her hand and led her to a chair.

"But that's quite ridiculous," Lise said. "Everything is ready: the paper and the ink and he's already written . . . It's quite ridiculous. Peter, it is quite, quite ridiculous." She sat down and she looked at her son and then at Pastor Holm and then at her son again. "Your father is dead, Peter," she said. Her voice was almost conversational. "Your father is dead."

She looked at him and then grasped his two arms and pulled him to her and pressed her face against him.

"Your father is dead, Peter," she said again.

21

"THE SILLY FOOL," LISE SAID CASUALLY. "HE COULD HAVE said something to save himself. He could have said something. The silly fool."

"Lise," Holm said patiently. "We now must make plans to remove you and Peter to Sweden." He had said this several times, and he knew it had made no impression at all upon her.

It was the evening of the next day. Pastor Holm and Gudrun sat bleakly in the rectory and listened to her. Peter stood silent. It was all something he had not yet grasped, not through all the afternoon before and the night and this day. It was not to be believed that someone could come there and in so many words say that his father was dead and already buried and now the only thing that was left was to take his body out of one hole in the ground and put it in another.

"The silly fool," Lise said again. She cupped her hands around a beaker of coffee, holding it as though it were a chalice. "The silly fool."

"Do you believe that, Lise?" Holm asked quietly.

"Of course I believe it," she said in the same random voice. "He could have given them something."

"Lise," the priest said.

"Is it better that he's dead?" she asked in the tone she might use to inquire the time of day. "Is that better? They said that his head looked like a big rubber ball before they were through with him."

"Lise!" the priest said sternly.

"Because of Peter?" she asked. "Peter must know this. Peter must never forget this. Like a big rubber ball. The silly, stupid, stubborn fool!"

"Lise, my child," Holm said, wondering as always, what can one say, what can one do? Pain is such a private thing that just to try to share it is an intrusion.

"The fool!" she said loudly. She jammed her knuckle into her mouth in sudden panic.

They had received the details of the death of Lars

Andersen from the prison doctor, a loyal Dane who had devoted his skills to trying to repair the damage done by the Gestapo interrogators, some of whom were quite clumsy, some who were not clumsy at all. It made no difference, the doctor had learned; in the end one could seldom tell whether the victim had been queried by a professional or an amateur.

The doctor had attempted an autopsy on Lars Andersen. But he had abandoned the automatic quest for the precise cause of death after locating three separate fractures of the skull, a fracture of the jaw, and, oddly, of the right arm. Most of the teeth had been broken or knocked out entirely.

The doctor had passed along to the Underground the additional information that until Lars Andersen had at last fallen dead from the chair to which at the end he had been bound to keep him erect, he had not opened his mouth except to occasionally voice pain.

"He died a brave man," Holm said, knowing the uselessness, the inanity of what he was saying. "The way a soldier dies, and for the same reason."

Lise looked up politely as if all of this in no way bored her and, to the same degree, in no way touched her. "Soldier? Like a soldier, did you say?" she looked at the priest with interest as though they were discussing some engaging item about the women's guild at the church. "Soldier? Do you mean they beat soldiers? They did that with their pistols, you know. Whipped him. Pistol-whipped. That's what the prison doctor said, wasn't it? Is that normal for soldiers?"

"Lise, you know what I'm trying to say to you. Lars did not tell them anything. He did not betray anybody."

"Of course not," Lise said, unsurprised. "He probably

138

was having a little laugh to himself thinking how proud we'd all be when he told us how strong he had been."

"I am proud of him," Peter said loudly.

She turned and gazed clearly at her son.

"I'm proud of my father. He could have had lots of people arrested if he talked," the boy said in a slightly lower voice.

"I know that, Peter," she said. She spoke to him in a voice she had not used in many years, in the voice she had used when he was much younger. "I'm proud of him too. But some people would have figured out something to tell them, anything to stall them, to buy a little time, anything at all. They're such fools, really, the Germans, they believe anything, especially if they've inflicted pain. The trouble with your father is that he was straight." She raised her head a little and brushed back a lock of hair that had fallen across her eyes.

"You see, Peter," she said in the same patient voice, "your father was straight and this is a crooked day and he couldn't even work out a few harmless lies so those German swine would leave him alone while they checked, leave him alone long enough for someone to help him. He had to keep his mouth shut and let himself be beaten to death. They said his head looked like a soccer ball before they were through with him, like a big soccer ball that had been kicked around for a long time."

"Lise," Pastor Holm said.

"I don't care," Peter said. "I'm glad."

"Glad that your father is dead?" Lise asked.

"You know I don't mean that," he said, and he said it not at all as the child she seemed to be speaking to. "But they probably would have killed him anyway. They would

139

have found out his lies and they would have killed him anyway and they would have hurt him more, and when he did die he would have died ashamed that he had bothered to lie instead of this way, proud that he didn't. Even if he was laughing to himself, as you say."

"He's right, Lise," Palle Holm said quietly.

She had listened to the boy, her eyes growing wide and wondering and soft, and when Peter was finished it was as though she had not heard the pastor at all, had not had to hear him. "Yes, Peter, you're right. And you know it. You knew it before I did, because you're his son."

"You haven't touched your coffee," Gudrun said for no reason. She was smoking the cigar the German Gestapo chief had left behind.

"No, I haven't touched my coffee," Lise agreed. "And it's real coffee smuggled from Sweden, and you were kind enough to make some for me tonight." She sipped from the cup.

"It must be cold now," Gudrun said.

"It's fine. It's really fine."

"Lise," Pastor Holm said.

"Yes, Palle," Lise said. "The coffee is delicious, Gudrun. Thank you very much. I know how scarce it is and how you come by it. It was lovely of you to fix some for me tonight."

"Lise," Holm said again.

"Yes, Palle, I'm listening and I'm quite all right now."

"We must get you and Peter away from here."

"If you say so, Palle. You have explained to me how we are all required to obey orders."

"Listen to me, Lise," Holm said, leaning forward, clasping his hands. "Gruber is no fool. His visit here was not just to question me about an explosion in some little factory. His agreeing to have a proper burial here—that was not an act of mercy."

"I did not think it was, Palle," Lise said. "Even in the curious state my mind is in now, that is not a quality I would associate with Major Gruber."

"They'll send Lars' body around tomorrow or the next day," Holm said tonelessly. "They'll be looking for you and Peter. Neither of you must be here.

"I would like to see my husband buried, Palle," Lise said.

"That means nothing," Holm said.

"That's an odd statement, coming from you, Pastor," Lise said.

Pastor Holm gripped his hands. "Lise, Lars Andersen died for one simple thing." He turned to his wife. "Gudrun, do you have to smoke that cigar?"

"No," his wife said. "I didn't think you minded."

"I don't mind. Only it reminds me too much of Major Gruber."

His wife put down the cigar.

"Lise," Holm continued. "Lars died so that his comrades would not get involved. He considered his life worth sacrificing for that simple purpose. Now those other people are quite numerous. They include me, and they include you, Lise; and they include Peter, and they include many people whose names would surprise you and others whose names would not surprise you at all. So there is no point in indulging yourself and by so doing make Lars Andersen's death that much less useful."

Lise set down the coffee cup as though it were made of the most fragile china and might shatter to pieces. "Indulge myself?" she asked. "Is that what you, a priest, call it? To be present at the burial of my husband?" She looked around and picked up a cigarette and lit it. "I will stay here until the ceremony is finished."

"Lise," Holm said.

"Useless, Pastor. Don't waste your breath."

Peter, who had been listening, looking from face to face as each person spoke, now said, "Pastor Holm is right."

"Peter, this is nothing for you to interfere in," Lise said without anger.

"It is something I can interfere in," Peter said boldly. "He was my father, and I want to be here too. But Pastor Holm is right. They'll be waiting here and they'll catch you and me both."

"I'm not afraid of them," Lise said, saying it as words.

"No?" Peter said. "I am. I'm afraid of them, Mother. And there's no point being silly. You're afraid of them too. We're all afraid of them. We'd be stupid not to be afraid of them. They hurt and they kill. But that isn't it, Mother. The thing is we can't let them catch us. Not now. Even if they didn't do what they did to my father. They can't catch us now."

"What is it you're trying to say?"

"The paper."

"The paper?"

"The last one my father wrote. We have to get that paper out."

"Out of the question," Pastor Holm said immediately. "My instructions are to get you both out of this house as soon as possible and get you underground and then out of the country. Quickly."

142

"Not until we print my father's last paper," Peter said.

"There is no time for that," Holm said.

Peter moved slightly away from his mother so that he seemed to be standing alone in the room. He stood very straight, his arms at his sides, his hands bunched into fists. "You cannot stop me, Pastor," he said.

"Peter!" Lise said.

"My father wrote that paper and it's the last thing he'll ever write, and I have the stencil and I won't tell anybody where it is. And I won't let you take me out of the country until that last paper is published and the people read the final things my father had to say. What was it he called it—his secret weapon, a time bomb? Well, that bomb is going to go off, even if he is dead." He turned swiftly to his mother and just as suddenly as he had changed he changed again. "I don't care, Mother, and you won't be able to stop me, either. Please, Mother, please."

Lise was silent for a long moment, and she looked at her son as though she were seeing him through new eyes. Then she said, "I wouldn't try to stop you."

"Lise," the priest said.

She put out the cigarette, again with great care. "No, Palle, I hadn't quite thought it out. But Peter did. Peter has said it. We cannot leave Denmark without this last statement from Lars Andersen."

"Lise, listen to me," Holm said.

"A kind of testament," Lise said evenly. "A kind of final testament from Lars Andersen, deceased."

"Lise, you don't know what you're saying," Holm said. "You must be reasonable."

143

Lise Andersen raised her lovely face, and on it there was a kind of light. "Whatever you put on his gravestone, Palle, whatever fine, memorable words you think up or I think up or anybody thinks up, they won't have any meaning. They won't have the meaning that is in that stencil Peter has put away—what a brave and clear thing to have done, Peter—because that is the valediction, those are the last words. Not what's carved upon stone but those words that came from his head and his heart and the love he had for Denmark and the decencies. The last words, Palle, the very last words, and they must not be lost. They must not die because he died. They must not be murdered the way Peter's father was murdered." She looked at Peter and then back at the priest. "You'd be as bad as they are, Palle," she said.

Presently Pastor Holm said, "I understand what you are saying, Lise. And I understand why, and I sympathize with you."

"The hell with your sympathy, Pastor Holm," Lise said evenly.

"I have received my instructions . . ."

"The hell with your instructions, Pastor Holm," Lise said.

"Lise, child . . ."

Lise lit another cigarette, and she was calm and in control. "Don't waste your time," she said as she had said before, only now she said it in a completely unemphatic manner. "I have to thank my son for seeing what I did not see. I have to thank you, Peter. You were quite right before, Palle. Staying here, watching you bury what was left of my husband after the Gestapo got through with him, was indulgence. Sheer, selfish indulgence, to give me solace, in no way to help my husband, because whatever it is you're going to put into the ground is not my husband, is not Peter's father. The only thing that is left of my husband outside of what is in my heart and what is in my son's heart is on that little stencil. That's a funny, odd, peculiar thing to leave behind, a little piece of inky paper with words cut into it by a typewriter, but my husband was a funny, odd, peculiar man. He was like that other man, that Spanish gentleman, the one who tried to fight windmills. He even looked like that man, and he fought his own windmills and he was struck down, but he had a few words to say, and they're going to be said the way he wanted them to be said." She turned again to Peter. "I'm beholden to you, Peter. For the rest of my life I'm beholden to you, and if God has taken away, He has also given in a way I could never have imagined."

There was a silence in the room. Pastor Holm, his hands still clasped, stared at the floor. Gudrun picked up the coffee server and poured Lise another cup of coffee. Lise took the cup and brought it to her lips and tried to drink from it, but it was as though that simple physical function possessed even by infants had been taken away from her, as though she had forgotten how to swallow. And then the cup dropped from her hands and fell upon her lap and the coffee spilled on her skirt and the steam rose and she felt nothing.

"Peter, Peter, help me," she said unhurriedly, although her shoulders were shaking. "God in heaven, Peter, help me. How shall we go on living without your father?"

The boy rushed to her, and she gripped his arms as though she were falling away somewhere and had only those arms to hold to.

"Mother," Peter said, fighting back tears. "Mother . . ."

She shook her head slowly. "No, no, no, no, Peter. There is nothing to listen to, because there is nothing to be said. He's dead, Peter. He's dead." She pulled him convulsively against her. "Your father is dead, Peter. Please help me."

22

THE HOSPITAL, THE SAME HOSPITAL WHERE LISE HAD fought her battle against pneumonia, was located on a small hill, and with its windows blacked out was only a darker shadow in the night.

The driver pulled up to an inconspicuous side entrance with no special instructions from Pastor Holm as though he had done that many times before, as he had.

Almost before they reached the door it was opened. A tall, slender, elderly deaconess in a severe habit greeted them.

"Pastor," she said. She stood back. "Mrs. Andersen. Peter." She glanced around outside. The taxi had moved off to a dark place, a darker place. When everyone was inside she shut the door. The corridor was dimly lit. "I'm very sorry, Mrs. Andersen."

"This is Sister Gerda," Pastor Holm said to Lise. "The superintendent."

"She knows?" Lise asked.

"She will hide you and Peter until we can manage to get you started for Sweden," the priest said.

"You and Peter can stay in my room for the moment,"

Sister Gerda said. Her face was thin and lined and her hair under her white cap was almost as white, but her eyes were bright.

"Sister," Lise said. "There is something you must know."

"There is nothing I need to know," the nun said.

"I must tell you this," Lise said.

"That you are in trouble? That the Germans may be looking for you?" She smiled, a melancholy smile that illuminated her austere face so that briefly everything was as shining as her eyes. "You do not think this is the first time I have had a visit from our pastor in the middle of the night. I count it a night lost when I don't see him, with someone or another."

"There is something I must tell you," Lise said again. She pointed to the blanket roll she had set upon the floor. "That contains sheets of paper, ink, mimeograph pads." She pointed to the bundle Peter still held slung over his shoulder. "That contains a mimeograph machine."

"Your husband's paper. We will have one more edition of it after all. How exciting! Will you run it off here?" Sister Gerda asked.

Lise looked at her wonderingly. "You don't mind? You're not afraid?"

Sister Gerda smiled again, a quite different smile. "I have been connected with this hospital for more than thirty years, Mrs. Andersen. I have seen everything that can happen in a hospital. Birth and death and pain and disease. I have seen miracles—miracles that have occasionally made me believe perhaps this man here has something." She looked at Pastor Holm. "Do you think the threat of Germans can frighten me?"

"No," Lise said at last. "No."

"Just let this vinegary old woman tell you what to do," Holm said, smiling at the nun. "Meanwhile, I'll get started on preparing some false identification papers for you." To the nun he said, "Is there anyone here who needs me?"

"Who would need you, you old fraud?" the nun said. "Pretending to be a pastor and all the time running around embarrassing our good friends who have come all the way from Germany to watch over us. Go on, run along, you old scoundrel, blow up a bridge somewhere and leave these people to me." She seemed taken with another thought. She turned to Lise, her eyes sparkling. "Mrs. Andersen, do you suppose I could help you with your paper?"

"You just watch yourself, Sister," Holm said.

"My heart? That funny business?" Sister Gerda waved her hand. "Fiddlesticks. It's as strong as yours."

"Bigger, anyway," Holm said.

Sister Gerda shook her head with pretended severity. "You must have had a very dull childhood, Palle Holm, to have to play games now. What have you got against Nazis anyway?"

Grinning, and actually, Peter thought, looking boyish, the priest put his hand on Lise's arm. "I shall be very close, Lise." He held out his hand to Peter. "Take care of your mother."

Peter took the hand and felt the strong grip. "Yes, sir. And thank you, sir."

"Thank me? Thank me for what, Peter?" He looked at Lise. "I'm sorry about all this."

"Sorry?"

The priest sighed. "The older I get the more I realize how inadequate I am. Or how inadequate words are."

"That's not what my father said," Peter said.

"No. But then he used them better than I do." He shook his head. "I don't know, but at times like these I feel I've chosen the wrong path in life."

"I should say," Sister Gerda said heartily. "What are you going to do with yourself when you have to stop playing games and have to go back to being a plain, ordinary clergyman again?"

"That's a good question," Holm said. He shrugged. "I have a feeling somehow I'll manage. Now good-bye, and I will see you all very soon."

"Off with you, Palle Holm. You two, come with me."

Lise picked up the blanket roll and walked behind the nurse. Peter followed them.

They walked down the darkened corridor. The hospital was very quiet. There was the hospital smell in the air, from the anesthetics and medicine. Other nurses passed them and glanced incuriously at the woman and the boy. No questions were asked. No greetings were given.

In this small hospital the staff lived in one part of the building and not in separate quarters. Sister Gerda led Lise and Peter down yet another corridor and up a flight of stairs. She stopped in front of the door and opened it.

"No one will disturb you here," she said as they entered the room. "You will be quite safe. I will bring you some coffee and cake."

She left, shutting the door behind her. Peter and Lise looked around. The room was small and sparsely furnished. There was a bed, a chair, a small dresser, a side-table next

149

to the bed, little else. On the wall was a single picture, a reproduction of a painting of a scene on the island of Bornholm.

Lise put the blanket roll on the floor and sat down slowly on the bed. Peter lowered his bundle and took the chair. They looked at each other without speaking.

Then Lise said, "It's so strange, isn't it?"

Peter nodded.

"Running away from our home, from our country, because of strangers who have no right to be here. What a world we live in."

"How is it, in Sweden?" Peter asked.

"You've been there."

"I can hardly remember."

"It is like our own country in many ways."

"They must be very brave, the Swedes."

"They are brave. They run a great risk taking all of us in."

"What makes people brave?"

"I don't know. It's something your father could have explained."

"My father was brave."

"He was very brave. He was too brave."

"You mustn't say that any more."

"I know," Lise said. "I know, Peter. It's all the good things, all the things to remember, all the things to be proud of, and if we live and this war ever ends, we shall be even more proud of it, remembering it." She bit her lip. "And yet, and yet, perhaps I would have chosen to be less proud and to have had your father remain alive."

"In his place I would rather die!" Peter said fiercely.

She looked at him with her tired eyes. "What do you know about dying, Peter?"

He did not answer her for a long while. Perhaps it was because he thought she did not really want an answer, was just asking one of those questions that need not be answered. Or perhaps it was because he was just coming to understand truly that his father was dead.

It had all happened so quickly and things happened fast upon each other after the Gestapo officer had left, that it had not sunk in, sunk in to be known and understood, the adjustment made to it, the accommodation that now was necessary. And when his mother asked him what she had just asked, it came to him that his father was dead, and there followed a staggering flow of thoughts of what that meant, what it meant now and what it meant for the future.

His father was dead, and it hit him like a kick in the belly.

He would never again see his father. He would never again listen to his father.

Lise, sensing what was going through Peter's mind, did not repeat the question. She looked at him sadly.

Then he raised his head. "Not very much," he said, answering her at last. "Not much at all. But what he did was right. Not just not saying anything to them when they were torturing him, not just that, but all the other things before that. Someday I'll want to know about those things —not only about the paper, but all the other things, the things the Germans wanted to find out and he didn't tell them. One day I'm going to make Pastor Holm tell me everything."

"Yes," she said. "It's all so simple to you, isn't it?"

Then she shook her head. "I'm sorry, Peter, I didn't mean that."

He thought again for a moment. "I don't know whether it's simple or not." Then he said, "It's funny. This is a hospital. There are sick people here. Some of them will die—nice people, but they'll die because they're sick, not for any other reason, just because they're sick, and the doctors couldn't make them well. I'm glad if my father had to die he didn't just die by accident that way."

Her eyes searched his face for a long time, and then she started to say something, but at that moment the door opened and Sister Gerda entered with a tray.

"I brought some chocolate," she said. "Now you drink this and eat something and don't worry. I shall be on duty at the front office, and if there is any kind of danger I'll wake you in good time." She went to the door. "Don't worry about any of the staff here," she said. "You can trust everyone, all of them. When the Nazis attempted their action against the Jews, we helped prevent it, even in our small way. Every Jewish patient in the hospital had his name changed overnight—on the records, his bed, everywhere. We passed almost a hundred of them through here during those days, and no one betrayed us."

Peter and Lise drank the hot chocolate and nibbled on the cookies and then they shoved the two blanket rolls under the bed. Lise said she would sleep in the chair and Peter would take the bed.

He refused flatly. "You take the bed, Mother," he said.

She knew there was no point arguing. For the moment their relationship had changed. She had neither the will nor the desire and, more importantly, not the strength to make him do anything he did not want to do. She lay down on the bed, fully clothed, and he drew a cover over her and kissed her good night and turned out the light.

He sat down in the chair in his overcoat. It was more silent than ever. He knew his mother was not sleeping but that she wanted him to think she was and he said nothing.

In the darkness, in the silence, he thought again how much had taken place, so rapidly, and he thought again how he would never be able again to speak to his father, to hear about herons and foxes, to see the tall, gangly man whose clothing always seemed a size too small for him, too short in the sleeves, too short in the trousers.

Was this how death struck? One way, and then quite suddenly in another, and nothing to be done about it? He had always thought vaguely that death had to be a noisy thing, something that made a commotion. At what moment had his father died? At what moment did all that made him a human being leave him, leave behind a body?

Somewhere in a box in the earth was a man whom he would hardly recognize, and what was in that box was all that was left on earth of his father.

23

IT WAS PECULIAR BECAUSE IT WAS ALL VERY LONG AGO, and he knew even now as he saw it again that he was dreaming, and yet in the dream he remembered things he had not remembered from the time they had happened—the time when his mother and father took him to Norway on a skiing holiday; and how very good his mother was on the skis, her small, compact body bent forward, leaning one way and then another; and how funny his father looked with his beanpole body and the skis getting twisted and his father falling down in the snow; and how he thought how simple it was the way his mother did it and how hard it was for his father and how, when he tried it himself, it was neither simple nor hard.

He remembered moving slowly, shuffling forward, carefully, and nothing bad happened, and nothing very good either. He just moved, on the beginners' run it was, and there was nothing memorable in any way. The good part was afterward when they went back to the lodge, and it was warm and there was a big fire and a lot of people were singing and he understood only part of the song because they were singing in Norwegian.

But the melody was a simple one, and pretty soon he was singing too and his father was singing in his scratchy voice that never seemed to hit the right notes. And somebody started a dance, a man and a woman, and then there were half a dozen couples dancing, and his mother was asked to dance by a Norwegian and his father nodded, and his mother learned the dance very quickly. She was so good at things like that, skiing and dancing and swimming, and his father always seemed to trip over himself no matter how hard he tried.

Except at the typewriter. Once Peter had come upon him as he was working on his portable typewriter in the living room. Peter started to speak, but then he didn't. He just watched the long, thin hands with the long, skinny fingers poised like the talons of a great bird over the keys of the machine. Then as the idea inside his father's head exploded, so did the long forefingers, for like most newspapermen, Lars Andersen typed with one finger of each hand, and the fingers went up and down like pistons, sailing over the keys, up and down, up and down, and the carriage rattled along; and then the long arm would reach out and the right thumb would catch the hook in the carriage and clatter it across the machine and the fingers would start their tattoo again.

There was perfect coordination of thought and action, of concept and transposition to paper, and once when Peter was taken to see the Royal Ballet, he was reminded of the time when he had watched his father work.

But on this skiing trip his father had fallen all over himself as usual. Peter remembered a man at the lodge with one leg in a plaster cast, and his father told him quite seriously that the man never skiied, that he had never been on skis in his life. He had this plaster cast all prepared and packed in his suitcase, and when he got to the skiing lodge he put on the cast and then went down to the big room on crutches and everybody sympathized with him, especially the girls, and he had a marvelous time.

Peter never found out whether his father was telling the truth or just teasing him. But the odd part of the dream was that all those things—the skiing, the lodge, the big fire, the people, the singing, the dancing, the man with the cast on his leg—all of those things his father had often told him had really happened. Only when his father told him that, in real life, he had never actually remembered it, but now in the dream that he knew while he was dreaming was a dream, he saw it all, exactly as his father had described it to him when he was trying to make him remember. He thought that when he woke he must tell his father he had actually seen it all in the dream. And then he heard the alarm clock ringing and he thought, while still asleep, that his father must be out of town on an assignment because the alarm clock usually was set only during those times. When his father was home he always woke Peter up himself, ruffling his hair.

He opened his eyes and reached out to turn off the alarm, and he sat up straighter. He did not remember the little room and the telephone rang again and he remembered. His mother was still asleep and he picked up the telephone and said, "Yes?"

"Sister Gerda here, Peter." The nun's voice was crisp. "There is a car coming up to the front entrance. A black car. It's burning petrol."

"Excuse me," Peter said, half asleep, still partly somewhere in Norway on a skiing holiday.

"Wake up, Peter," the nun said. "I think we are going to have some German visitors."

The words came quietly, unhurriedly over the telephone, and then they all came together, and all Peter could think of first was that he would never be able to tell his father about the dream, and then he said, "What shall we do, Sister?"

"Listen to me carefully, Peter," Sister Gerda said calmly. "Just push the two blanket rolls under my bed, back against the wall. You and your mother remain where you are, just stay there. Whatever is going to happen will take a little time; there are many rooms and wards here. Do you understand? Just hide the blanket rolls and keep yourselves alert and I'll ring you again and tell you what to do, in the event you have to do anything. Do you understand?"

"Yes, Sister."

"It may be nothing at all, but best to be prepared."

"Yes, Sister."

He hung up, knowing it would not be nothing at all; he had grown up that much. It was never nothing at all, not these days; then he touched his mother's hand.

"Mother," he whispered. "Wake up."

His mother opened her eyes and was instantly awake.

"Sister Gerda," he said in the same whisper. "She just rang here. A car is pulling up to the hospital. She thinks it's the Germans."

His mother, lying in the bed still, began to tremble. She looked at her watch. The luminous dial showed it was just after 4:30 in the morning. She sat up, pulling down her dress, and looked at the watch again.

"Are you all right?" Peter asked.

"Yes, Peter."

"She said to put the things back up against the wall under the bed and then just to wait for her to call again, if she has to call again. She said it might be nothing to do with us."

Lise nodded. Peter got down on his knees and pushed the two blanket rolls against the wall. When he stood up, his mother was still seated on the bed, her hands clasped, trembling.

"Don't worry, Mother," he said.

"No, Peter, of course not."

"Sister Gerda didn't seemed worried."

"No." Then she said, "Peter, I'm frightened. It seems easier if I say it."

He nodded. Then he frowned because he discovered he was not frightened. Not the way his mother was. The

157

fact that she was frightened and said so took some of it away from him. He wondered why that was. Was it there was only so much fear to go around? That couldn't be it. Whatever there was of fear, there was enough for both of them.

"I had such a funny dream," he said, feeling he must say something. He could not bear to watch his mother shake that way.

"It's just that I'm tired, Peter," Lise said. "I'd be frightened anyway, of course, but I'm tired and that always makes it worse. You understand?"

"Yes, Mother. This dream. It was about the time we all went skiing in Norway, and I remembered it all in the dream, even the way you were dancing in the lodge."

"Did you? I remember that time."

The door opened and Sister Gerda slipped into the room, breathing a little faster than normal. "Gestapo," she said. Her eyes, Peter could see even in the dim light, were sparkling again.

"You mustn't run that way," Lise said.

"Fiddlesticks. Now listen. There is no problem keeping out of their way. They're so methodical, and it's quite simple in a place like this. The only thing is you mustn't panic."

"We won't," Peter said.

"You can avoid them," Sister Gerda said. "I'll stall them. Then just listen for them. They clump like oxen. I keep telling them to be quiet, not to disturb the patients, but they never pay any attention. Just listen for them and keep out of their way and then come back to this room."

"Yes, Sister," Peter said.

"Did they ask about us?" Lise asked.

"They never say." Sister Gerda raised her hands in a contemptuous gesture. "They just try to look mysterious, and all they do is look stupid. Germans! They make me want to laugh in their faces."

That was a new thought to Peter. He had never heard of anyone who wanted to laugh at the Gestapo.

"Have you hidden all those things?" the nun asked.

"Under the bed, against the wall," Peter said.

"Good. Now remember, don't panic. If you keep your heads, everything will sort itself out. Every sister in the hospital stands ready to help you." She turned to the door. "This is exciting. Those men! Caricatures!" She threw up her hands again. "Germans!"

She rushed out of the room, and they could hear her walking rapidly down the corridor. Peter remembered what Pastor Holm had said about her having something the matter with her heart.

"I think we'd better move out of here," Peter said.

"You lead the way, Peter," Lise said.

Peter opened the door and looked up and down the dimly-lit corridor. It was empty and silent. He beckoned to his mother, and they stepped out of the room. Peter took her hand and led her down the corridor in the direction away from Sister Gerda's office. They walked to the end of the corridor and started to turn into another corridor when suddenly Peter stopped.

"What is it? Did you hear something?" Lise asked. She started to tremble again.

"The things in the blanket. In Sister Gerda's room," Peter said.

"What about them?"

"They may search her room. If they think we're here,

then they'll know she must know about it and they may look in her room."

"Do you believe that?" Lise asked, in exactly the same way she would have asked Lars.

"We'd better get the things out," Peter said. "If they catch us, it doesn't matter whether we have them or not."

Lise nodded and they ran back to Sister Gerda's room. They both got down on their knees and crawled under the bed together. One of the blanket rolls, the one containing the paper and ink and pads, opened up as they pulled it out and all the things scattered on the floor. They gathered them together quickly, and then suddenly Lise laughed.

Peter turned to her in surprise.

Lise rested on her elbows under the bed and giggled. "I just thought," she said, still giggling. "I just thought how funny it would be if they came into the room now and found us both under the bed."

She shook her head and laughed some more and Peter realized it was not funny laughing. "Stop, Mother," he said.

She stopped instantly. "I must be losing my mind," she said.

They finally got everything gathered together and rolled up again, and they crawled out from under the bed. Each of them now carrying a blanket roll, they ran out of the room and down the corridor. They turned into the other corridor and saw that at the end of that corridor were glass doors. They could see a nurse seated at a desk looking at them through the glass doors.

They paused for a moment and then they heard footsteps behind them and they ran to the glass doors. The nurse, Peter saw when they pushed through the door, was very old, older by far than Sister Gerda. She was in a nun's habit and she was very small, almost lost in the chair behind her desk.

Peter looked at her for a moment and then said, "Gestapo. I think they're looking for us."

The old nurse pointed a small finger. "That room is empty. Get in there."

Peter and his mother ran into the room and closed the door. They stood inside the door, breathing so heavily Peter thought surely they could be heard by anyone passing. He made his mother move back into the room, but he kept his own ear against the door.

Presently he heard the footsteps. Sister Gerda was right, he thought, his heart starting to beat faster, they do clump like oxen, and he remembered the time in Tivoli when they were looking for him there. The footsteps passed. They waited. Presently they saw the knob on the door being turned slowly. Peter backed away. The old nurse stuck in her head. She beckoned with one of her tiny fingers.

She led them down the corridor a few yards and then into another room across the hall. She chuckled. "They searched this room," she whispered. "They're so orderly. Up one side and down the other."

She put her finger to her lips and closed the door and Peter and his mother waited; soon they heard the footsteps again, heavy as before, and the opening and closing of doors. Then there was silence.

They waited. It seemed a very long time to Peter, although Lise stood motionless, ignoring the chair in the room, ignoring the passing of the minutes as well.

There was the sound of footsteps again, but these were not the clumps of oxen. The door opened.

Sister Gerda said, "They're gone."

24

"THE IDEA CAME TO ME FROM THE RIFLE RANGE," Sister Gerda explained.

"Excuse me, Sister?" Peter said politely.

"The way they trained the Resistance people. Pastor Holm told me all about it." Sister Gerda looked at them brightly.

Peter, Lise, and the superintendent were in a small room just off the main office of the hospital. In the larger office, girls were working busily, keeping records and files up to date, answering telephones, typing. It was Sister Gerda's idea to set up the mimeograph machine in the small office.

"It seems to be so public," Lise said doubtfully.

"That's just it," Sister Gerda said. "That's the point." And then she said what she had said about the rifle range, which seemed incomprehensible.

"What about the rifle range?" Peter asked.

"Pastor Holm told me all about it," the nun said again. "It's supposed to be a secret, I guess, but it happened some time ago, and the boys don't need that kind of training now. They have enough real life targets, I guess. But what happened was that they had to teach a great many young men, boys most of them, how to handle rifles and that meant shooting, and there seemed to be no place to go because it also meant a lot of noise, and the Germans always investigate that kind of noise. Anyway, it was somebody's idea, I don't know exactly whose, to set up a rifle range right next door to the German rifle range."

"Of all places," Lise said.

Peter started to laugh. "There was so much shooting on the German range the sounds all got mixed up."

"Exactly," Sister Gerda said, triumphant in having made her point. "That's what gave me the idea." She waved her hand toward the outer office. "This is a big, busy place, with lots of people working. What could be more natural than that someone should be operating a mimeograph machine?"

"I'm not sure," Lise said.

"She's right, Mother," Peter said. "It's a marvelous idea. I read a story about something like that once, by an American writer, about a stolen letter and how it was left among a lot of ordinary letters and nobody bothered looking for it there."

Lise, still unconvinced, deferred to him as she was coming to do more and more. The little machine had been put on a small table in the smaller office. The paper was taken there with all the other things needed to get out the newspaper.

"That appears to be a great many sheets of paper," Sister Gerda said.

"Five thousand," Peter said.

"That many?" the nun asked, astonished.

"And what a time my mother had finding this paper," Peter said. "And the ink, and everything else. That's why we can't let it all go to waste. Right, Mother?"

Lise nodded.

"That will take a great deal of time," Sister Gerda said.

"Not too long."

"In any case, we'll all help," the nun said. "I'll help too." The sparkle appeared in her eyes. "I've never helped get out an illegal paper. This is all quite exciting."

Lise, who had operated the machine far more often than Peter, fixed the stencil onto the roller. Then she inked the pad. She turned the crank to run off the first sample copy. Halfway through the crank jammed.

"Let me see," Peter said. He inspected the machine and found the trouble quickly. One of the metal supports holding the roller had been knocked out of line and had bent a bar turing a gear.

"It must have happened in moving it," Lise said. "What do we do now?"

"There's a handyman in the hospital," Sister Gerda said. "He may be able to set it to rights."

"No," Peter said. "We need a machinist."

"Where in heaven's name will we find one of those?" Lise asked. She sat down and brushed her hand across her face. "Your father would have known where to go, but for the life of me, I can't think." She lowered her eyes and rubbed her face again. "I can't seem to think much these days about anything."

"I know where to go," Peter said.

Lise looked up. "You do? Where?"

"Kai Madsen's father has a machine shop," Peter said.

"Your friend, your school friend?"

"His father fixed my bicycle once and wouldn't take any money."

"Do you think we can trust him?" Lise asked.

164

"Kai Madsen's father? Of course we can trust him," Peter said. "I told you, Kai is a good friend of mine."

"Is his father a good Dane?" Lise asked.

"Yes, Mother."

"Where is his shop?"

"In Snekkersten."

"Where in Snekkersten?"

"I know where it is," Peter said.

"But I have to know if I'm going to take the machine there."

"I'll take it."

Lise looked up sharply. "I think not, Peter. It's too much risk."

"It's more risk for you," he said. "They'd recognize you before they would me."

"He's right," Sister Gerda said.

After a moment Lise nodded. "All right," she said tonelessly. "All right."

"I'll have to wrap it in something," Peter said looking around. "That blanket wouldn't look too well."

Sister Gerda put her finger to her lips. "What about a laundry bag?"

"Perfect," Peter said.

The nun got a white bag and Peter slipped the machine into it. Lise suddenly reached out and took his hand.

"Peter, listen to me," she said. There was life and urgency in her voice now. "Listen to me. Forget the machine and printing the paper. Just let them get us away from here."

"Mother!"

She gripped his hand harder. Her face and her eyes

165

were exhausted and filled with sudden terror. "Peter, after all, one more edition, one small paper, going to a few thousand people, after all what does it really matter? Peter, let's just chuck this away somewhere and let Pastor Holm get us away from here."

Peter shook his head. "No, Mother."

Lise looked wildly at the nun. "Tell him, Sister, tell him I'm right. It's what Pastor Holm wanted to do in the first place. We're running such a risk, and we're endangering people here, and for what? It's all so useless, Peter. There are so many Germans, and they're stronger than we are. It's all so useless."

Peter took his hand away from his mother's. "My father didn't believe that."

"No he didn't," Lise said bitterly. "And your father is dead."

"All the more reason to prove that he didn't die for nothing," Peter said.

Now Lise took the nun's hand and pressed it against her cheek. Her eyes filled with tears. "Sister, Sister, tell him. Tell him I'm right. I don't have the strength any more. Tell him the sensible thing, the reasonable thing, is for us just to forget all about this and get away—get away somewhere where there are no Germans, no Gestapo."

"I can't do that, Mrs. Andersen," Sister Gerda said quietly. "Everything you say may be right . . ."

"It's the only sensible thing to do," Lise cried.

"These are not sensible times, Mrs. Andersen," the nun said. "I knew of Lars Andersen and I knew of this paper and I couldn't wait each week to read it, and if he has prepared a final edition, then it must be published."

166

Peter waited until early afternoon, for the time when school would normally be finished for the day, so he would not look conspicuous on the streets, and then he set out.

"Be careful," Lise said. Her eyes were dull.

"Don't worry. I won't let this get damaged again."

"I don't mean the machine, Peter," Lise said.

"Don't you think he knows that, Mrs. Andersen?" Sister Gerda asked.

It was a dark, gray day and there was the smell of more snow in the air. Peter walked from the hospital with the bag under his arm.

The station at Elsinore was neither more nor less crowded than usual and he sat down and waited quietly for the train. When it came, he got on and rode to Snekkersten. It seemed strange to be in his own little village again. Snekkersten looked different. He could not see how nor why, but it seemed quite a different place. As he walked down the street, he realized that the change was in him and that the few days that had passed since he had last been there were days that had divided his life.

He saw only the usual number of Germans in uniform as he walked to the small machine shop that was on a winding road leading up from the Sound. Kai Madsen's father, Ole, was dealing with a customer when Peter entered the shop. Peter waited quietly until the customer was gone.

Ole Madsen, a brawny man who in another time might have been the blacksmith in the village, looked at Peter. "What can I do for you, young man?"

"Do you remember me, Mr. Madsen?"

Madsen peered at him. Then he said, "Come into the back." He looked over Peter's shoulder. "Did anybody see you come here?"

"I don't think so, sir," Peter said.

In the back of the shop, Madsen took the mimeograph machine out of the bag. "Is this what your father used?"

"Yes, sir."

"Why are you bothering about this now?"

"My father typed one last stencil."

Madsen raised his eyes under his bushy, fair brows. "But he's dead, lad."

"I'm going to print the paper," Peter said.

Madsen nodded as though this did not surprise him. "I won't ask you where. I know the Germans have been asking about your mother and you. You know that?"

"Yes, sir."

Madsen bent over the machine. "Nothing much wrong here," he said. "I'll fix it for you in a jiffy. Do you want something to eat?"

"No, sir."

"Then just sit down there and wait. One more of Lars Andersen's little papers. Well, isn't that something. I'm going to miss that paper." He started dismantling the roller. "We'll all miss it, lad. Your father was a fine man." He started to work with a small wrench and screwdriver.

"Yes, sir," Peter said.

"Kai misses you."

"Yes."

"I guess you won't be going back to school. Not for a while." He worked rapidly and skillfully. "What a time. Boys being driven from school. But then I don't suppose that makes you too unhappy."

"I'll catch up," Peter said.

"Of course you will. So you're going to get out the paper."

168

"Yes, sir."

"Your father would like that, lad. Your mother, how is your mother?"

"All right."

"Poor woman. Tell her how sorry I am. Tell her how sorry we all are. War. What a stupid business. And what does it settle? People getting killed. Things getting destroyed. And then it's all over, and nothing has been settled."

"My father always said something would be settled this time," Peter said.

Madsen looked up. His eyes were very blue under the fair brows. "He did, did he? Well, he should know more than I. That was his business. Perhaps he was right. Perhaps this is one of the wars that has got something to be settled after all. That Hitler. What an unpleasant man. I heard him on the radio once. He must be crazy, screaming and shouting like that, for heaven's sake."

Peter watched anxiously as Madsen took the machine apart. He watched as the machinist straightened the supporting post and rod and threw away the damaged gear. He fished around in a big drawer until he found another gear that fit, and he put the machine together again. He gave the handle a crank and the roller went round without resistance.

"There," he said. "Good as new. Better. They don't make things the way they used to, nothing. I can tell you that. But this is shipshape now. There."

"I don't have any money," Peter said. "Just train fare. I'll have to owe you for this."

Madsen's brows bunched fiercely. "Owe me? No money? And you waited until now to tell me."

169

"I only realized it when you were working on it," Peter said. "But I'll sign a paper. I'll pay you."

Madsen slammed a hand as big as a ham on the work table. He growled, "Did you think I'd take money if you had it?"

"No," Peter said.

"Then why did you mention it?"

"I couldn't just say nothing."

Madsen glared at him for a moment and then put the machine back into the laundry bag. He handed the bag to Peter. "I'll tell Kai you were here."

"Yes," Peter said. "And thank you."

"Mind, watch yourself. Those damned Germans are as thick as thieves these days. Makes me think of flies in a stable in summer."

"Yes, sir."

"I'll tell Kai."

"Tell him I'll be seeing him one of these days," Peter said.

25

THEY STARTED RUNNING OFF THE PAGES AS SOON AS PETER returned. Sister Gerda helped with great pleasure. She read one of the papers and was flabbergasted at the story concerning Major Gruber. When Lise explained Lars Andersen's humor and his intent, the nun burst into laughter. She laughed so hard she had to sit down and wipe her eyes.

They got through about half of the run when they

decided to call it quits for the night. The finished papers were wrapped into brown paper bundles, tied and hidden in one of the hospital filing cases.

They had hot chocolate and a piece of cake and they went to their rooms. Both Lise and Peter were now duly registered as patients at the hospital. They were carried on the records as Vibeke Juel, a cardiac case, and Rolf Damm, suffering from an obscure blood ailment.

Peter undressed and got into bed. He was happy with the way the day had gone, and he fell asleep immediately. He was wakened during the night by Sister Gerda, who seemed never to sleep. She put a finger to her lips and whispered, "Pastor Holm is here."

Peter sat up. "What's the matter?"

"He's with your mother. Get dressed."

Peter slipped into his clothes and followed Sister Gerda as she hurried to her own room. Peter went into the room and then stopped in astonishment.

Lise was seated in a chair. A nurse was busy cutting her long hair.

"What's happening?" he asked.

Pastor Holm stepped forward and put his arm around the boy. "A little trouble, Peter," he said in his deep voice.

Lise looked up. "They've blown up our house."

"What!"

Holm nodded. "Germans. They couldn't just ransack the house like ordinary human beings, although I'm sure they did that first. They dynamited it."

"But why?" Peter asked.

"If we knew why, we might know a great deal," Pastor Holm said. "We might know why Nazis are Nazis. In any case, you both must move. Whatever is in those Gestapo minds, it's a warning, plain enough. They won't rest until they find you."

Peter was staring at his mother. Her dark hair, which she sometimes had worn in the old-fashioned manner, plaited and twisted into a roll on top of her head, now was cropped into a close bob.

Lise smiled. "Do I look funny, Peter?"

"Why are you doing that?"

"Melodrama, lad, melodrama," Holm said. He gave a short laugh. "At a time like this it always seems like a bad film."

The nurse cut off the last of the hair and then began to apply a liquid from a bottle.

"We were lucky," Holm said. "Sister Asta here used to work in a beauty establishment before she decided to take up a more useful life. And fortunately our good Sister Gerda remembered that as she seems to remember everything else."

Before Peter's eyes, as though the room were a dressing room in a theater, his mother was transformed from one woman to another. The hair was turned blonde, the eyelashes were lightened.

"There," Holm said. "There. I can hardly recognize you."

"What about Peter?" Lise asked.

"We can't do much about Peter," the priest said. "We can't give him a false beard. We can't even shave off a moustache." He rubbed his chin. "I'm afraid most twelve-year-old boys look more or less alike, especially in this country, and we'll have to trust that."

When Sister Asta was finished, she stepped back and surveyed her work.

"Fine," the pastor said. "Fine. You'd fool anyone, Lise. Now you remember the name and address I gave you?"

"Yes, Palle."

"He's a good man, a lawyer, and he has agreed to hide you until we can move you again. Now just leave here as though you were being discharged from the hospital and go directly to his home."

"What about the machine and the rest of the paper?" Peter asked.

"I'll take care of all that," Holm said. "And I'll see that the paper goes where it should go."

"But we're only half finished," Peter said.

"Half will have to do this time."

Peter backed away slowly. "No, sir."

"Peter," Lise said. "We've got most of the pages printed."

"Half," Peter said. "Half isn't most."

"We'll have to be satisfied with that."

He shook his head stubbornly. "We have to finish it."

"Peter," Lise said. "There's no time to argue about this now."

Holm walked over to the boy. "Peter, there wouldn't even be this much done, if you hadn't insisted," he said gently. "But you must listen now. It's too dangerous to attempt any more. You and your mother must go underground now, properly underground, and you must do exactly as you are told."

"We have to print the other half," Peter said.

"Peter, for heaven's sake!" Lise said sharply.

Pastor Holm half raised his hand to stop her. He looked at Peter for a long time, and then he put his hand

173

on his shoulder. "I knew your father from the time he was your age. He was the most stubborn boy I ever knew and he grew up into the most stubborn man."

"I won't go until we're finished," Peter said. He felt his lip quivering and he fought to hold it still.

"Of course you won't," Holm said. "And with God's help you shall not."

In the darkness of the winter morning Sister Gerda accompanied Lise and Peter out of the hospital. Peter and his mother again were carrying blanket rolls. A taxi was waiting for them.

Sister Gerda walked down the steps to the taxi.

"Go back," Lise said. "It's so cold."

The taxi driver hopped out and opened the door. He looked curiously at the blanket rolls.

"Yes," Sister Gerda said. "It's so sad, the little one dying. Are you certain you want to bother taking all her belongings with you? Wouldn't it be better if you just left them? No, of course not. Well, good-bye and God bless you."

The cab drew away. Peter and Lise turned and looked back. Sister Gerda waved to them and then walked back into the hospital.

26

MAJOR GRUBER TOOK A COMFORTABLE PUFF ON HIS CIGAR. "The question, Sister, is simply this: who is Vibeke Juel and who is Rolf Damm?"

"I have told you," Sister Gerda said patiently. "They were patients here."

The Gestapo officer tapped the record book with a thick, manicured finger. "So it states here. But who are they and, more importantly, where are they now?"

"I cannot follow all my patients to their homes, Major."

"I did not come here to listen to humor, Sister," Gruber said.

"I am not trying to be humorous," Sister Gerda said. She stood in front of the German officer, her arms folded. She had been questioned for some time now and she was tired, but she would not sit down. She would not give the Gestapo that.

"Of course you cannot follow each patient home," Gruber said tolerantly. "But I can."

He peered at the ledger. "Yesterday seven persons were discharged from this hospital, including a Vibeke Juel and a boy named Rolf Damm, who is listed here as being of the age of twelve. Now it has been quite simple for me to verify the names and addresses of five of these persons, to verify that they are indeed at their homes, recovering nicely from a variety of ailments due to the excellent treatment they received here. But I can find no trace of a Vibeke Juel or a Rolf Damm. The addresses listed here are fictitious."

"That is no fault of mine, Major," Sister Gerda said calmly. "It also is impossible for me to check on every home address patients give me."

"That is understandable," Major Gruber said reasonably. "You must understand I am aware of that. But it so happens, Sister, that I am looking for a woman in her early thirties and for a boy about twelve. And it also happens you have registered here the names of a woman, let me see . . ." He looked at the record book again, although he had studied it carefully before. ". . . Aged thirty-four, and the boy, twelve." He raised his eyes to the superintendent. "Isn't that a curious coincidence?"

"I don't know what it is, Major," Sister Gerda said. She touched her eyes. "I cannot tell you any more than I have. If people want to give us false names and addresses for reasons of their own, that is something we cannot control."

"That is not exactly true, Sister," Gruber said. He stood up and took a few steps back and forth. "Sister, I know you must be very tired, but there is an urgency here. You must understand that." He paused and looked at her. His eyes were blue and sharp. "You do understand?"

"Yes, Major."

"Now, what about identity cards?"

"What about them, Major?"

Gruber held up his hands. "People have them. They are required to have them. It is quite simple to verify names."

Sister Gerda breathed deeply. "Major, we are very thinly staffed here. There is a great deal of work and too few people to do it. When someone comes in here ill and tells us his name, we just put that down, and we don't usually ask him to prove he is who he says he is."

Gruber nodded as though that made sense to him. He walked back to where the ledger was lying on the desk and looked at it again. Then he straightened and turned to the nun with a pleasant smile. "A cardiac case and an unspecified blood ailment. I would like to see some of the charts showing the treatment given to these patients."

Sister Gerda closed her eyes and said nothing.

"A cardiac case and a blood ailment," Gruber mused. "Both patients are here approximately seventy-two hours. They come together. They leave together. And I gather there are no records of any medical treatment while they are here. It's all such an unfortunate coincidence. You must admit it is quite curious."

"It is anything you want it to be, Major," Sister Gerda said, and now, despite her will, she could not keep the exhaustion out of her voice.

"I would like nothing more than to believe you, Sister," Gruber said sympathetically. "I would like just to be able to thank you and tell you to go and get some rest. I am sure that with all your activities here you must need it. But I'm afraid it is quite impossible. I must know more about these two mysterious people."

"I can tell you nothing more."

Gruber nodded. "Not here, perhaps, in your own office. But it might be different in my office. Somehow people discover an atmosphere there that persuades them to answer questions. They seem to remember more there."

The elderly nurse nodded. "I'll fetch my cloak, Major."

"Becker!" Gruber said.

A Gestapoman sprang to attention. "Yes, Herr Major!"

"Accompany the sister to her quarters."

Sister Gerda's face, white with exhaustion, broke into a faint smile. "I shall not try to escape, Major."

177

"But of course not. Still rules are rules and regulations are regulations, and a prisoner must be accompanied by a guard."

"Then I am to consider myself a prisoner?" the nurse asked.

"Just a technicality, Sister. Soon after we arrive at my headquarters, you will tell me everything I want to know." He puffed on his cigar. "Then we will decide how we must deal with you."

Her head erect, Sister Gerda walked out of her office, past the girls working in the larger office, followed by the Gestapoman. The girls glanced up and then quickly went back to their work.

Gruber broke the ash from his cigar and wandered out after her. The girls glanced at him and again applied themselves to their routine work. He roamed around the large office, looking at this and that. He pulled open a file drawer, thumbed idly through it, closed it, and opened another. He pushed that closed, knocked some ash from his cigar, looked with pleasant interest at some of the more attractive girls, strolled over to another file, opened it and closed it. He glanced at his watch and pulled open still another file.

He was about to slide the file shut when he looked again. In the deep drawer he saw several small packages wrapped in brown paper, tied neatly with string.

He took a small penknife from his pocket and cut the string on the top package and opened it. He extracted a sheet of paper. He read what was printed on the paper. He frowned, puzzled for a moment, and then his eyes darkened.

"Braun," he said.

Another Gestapoman came to attention. "Yes, Herr Major."

"See what is delaying the sister."

"That is not necessary," a man's voice said.

Gruber turned. A doctor in a long white coat was coming in from the corridor. The girls stopped their work.

"Where is she?" Gruber asked. The office was very still.

"She was not young, Major," the doctor said. "And she was not well. She needed to lie down and rest."

"Braun, go and bring that woman here," Gruber said.

"Major, you don't seem to understand," the doctor said quietly. "Sister Gerda had to lie down and rest. Unfortunately for you, it is a rest that not even the Gestapo can disturb."

Gruber raised the cigar to his lips and then lowered it without drawing on it. He carefully folded the sheet of paper he had read and slipped it into his coat pocket.

"Braun," he said.

"Yes, Herr Major."

"The packages in this drawer. You will take them down to the furnace and burn them."

"Yes, Herr Major."

"You will remain there until you are certain they are in ashes."

27

"YOU MUST BE TERRIBLY TIRED," LISE SAID. "HERE, LET ME crank that for a while."

"No," Peter said.

"I know how, you know," she said drily.

He looked up at her and grinned. He couldn't get used to her with blonde, short hair. "I'm not tired," he said.

It was that, but it was more than that, and it was nothing he could tell her about, not now. They were in the lawyer's house, and it was the second night they were there. They couldn't do anything the first night because the lawyer wouldn't let them. Then the lawyer had gone somewhere, on business he said—he was just plain scared, Lise said—and on the second night they had gone to work.

And somehow, turning the crank of the machine, it became something else to Peter. It became many things. It first was a sword he was swinging against enemies, and when his wrist got tired and his fingers cramped, he breathed a little deeper and continued to fight those who opposed him.

He remembered a word, a Finnish word, his father had once told him about. *Sisu.* It was a Finnish quality, his father had said. It was hard to translate, but roughly it meant: when you couldn't go on any more, you found the strength somewhere and went on. *Sisu.*

As the hours passed and his mother stacked the pages, it was as though Peter was possessed. For it stopped being a Viking sword he was swinging and it became a mace he was smashing against the armor of his foe. It became a cudgel and a quarter staff and a heavy bayonetted rifle he was not shooting but swinging and jabbing with might and main. The people he was fighting were the people his father had fought, the people who in the end had killed his father, but who stupidly had left behind someone who could pick up the weapons and continue the fight.

180

He could not explain all that to his mother, not yet, because even to himself it was silly—a little ordinary mimeograph machine and imagining so much about it, but somewhere inside him it didn't seem so silly and when his muscles ached and his eyes got heavy, the imagining helped. *Sisu.*

He could not explain that to his mother nor could he explain why he could not let her operate the machine. Not now. Not just now.

After a while she lay down on a sofa and slept, an odd-looking blonde woman who was his mother, and he kept working the machine, a guard on night duty now, alone. Why were all those stupid thoughts passing through his mind? His father always said he had a vivid imagination. Was that what it was? Could it mean that he had thoughts the way his father had had thoughts, that that was the way his mind worked, that he could imagine things and perhaps put them down on paper, that he might—and he felt a new rush of excitement and *sisu*—one day be a writer too?

It would be too much. He had not thought too much about what he wanted to be when he was a man. Or rather he had thought of a dozen things, and they all changed with the years, the seasons, a new film, a new book.

But this seemed different. He was making word pictures in his mind. And words were weapons, his father had said, the most powerful, the most dangerous weapons.

It would be something, wouldn't it?

He spoke to his father silently and asked his opinion, and it pleased him to think in that early hour of the morning with his different blonde mother sleeping deeply and his own eyes begging to close, it pleased him to think his father made that funny face he used to make and nodded.

When Pastor Holm arrived shortly after six o'clock in the morning, Lise was still sleeping and Peter was tying up the last of the bundles.

"I finished them, Pastor," the boy said. His voice had all the exhaustion and all the elation.

Then he saw the expression on the priest's face.

"What is it, Pastor?" he asked.

Holm was at Lise's side, waking her gently. She saw it in the priest's face too.

"What is it?" she asked quickly, sitting up. She was completely awake, the quick wakefulness of the hunted.

"Sister Gerda," Holm said. "May God rest her soul."

"Oh, my God," Lise said.

"But she waved good-bye to us," Peter said.

Quickly the priest told them what had happened, and as he spoke Lise put her knuckle in her mouth as she had when she had heard her husband was dead, and when Holm finished she said, "We did it."

"You must not think that, Lise," the priest said.

"But we did, Palle," Lise said. "You told us about her heart. It was us. Gruber would never have gone there but for us."

Holm stood up and looked at her sternly. "Lise, Sister Gerda is dead. But you must not in any way feel guilty."

"We are guilty," Lise said.

"Yes," Peter whispered.

Holm shook his head. "Sister Gerda had been ill for a long time. She was told by every doctor in the hospital to stop working—not just to rest, not just to take it easier, but to stop, to retire. And she refused and they knew it would kill her sooner or later, and she knew it as well. She had a long and giving life, and the only thing she was worried about was that one day she would not be of use."

"Words," Lise said.

"It happened because of us," Peter said.

"You are not listening to me, neither of you," Holm said harshly. "I am telling you Sister Gerda died as she wanted to die, working until the very last minute of her life."

"The Gestapo came because of us," Lise said.

"The Gestapo was there almost every day of the week, always questioning, poking around, checking," Holm said in the same rasping voice. "If a man hurt his hand working, burned himself, broke a leg, they were there, trying to find out if he was a saboteur doing something they call illegal. Sister Gerda fought with the Gestapo in her own way for four years, and she died fighting them." Holm paused and then he said very quietly, "I am a priest, and I try to serve our Lord as best I can, and I pray only that I may die as she did, working for what she believed in until the very last minute."

The room was still. Then Holm said, "It is the time, my dear friends, and we didn't make the time, or perhaps we did, and we must live with it."

Then unexpectedly he smiled. "Now I will tell you something that should make you feel better. You were right, Peter, and we were wise to listen to you."

Peter looked at him questioningly.

"You see," the priest went on, "while waiting for Sister Gerda, to take her to Gestapo headquarters, our good Major Gruber poked around in the files."

"The paper," Peter said quickly.

Holm nodded. "The paper. He found the bundles and he opened one of them and he read the paper and it seems he quite understood. He had all the papers burned —except one copy which he kept, apparently to amuse him in his old age." Holm's smile was almost devilish now and his big, red apple cheeks almost closed his eyes. "You see, Major Gruber now believes he has destroyed the entire issue—that the little story intended to do him harm is his secret. But we know better."

Peter looked at his mother, who was quietly crying. He went to her and took her hand.

"You two must move on," Holm said. "But I will give you this promise. This batch of Lars Andersen's newspaper will not be burned. These pages will be distributed today, and if there are only half the usual number, why then people will pass them around just twice that much more."

28

THE TAXI DRIVER STOOD IN FRONT OF MAJOR GRUBER'S DESK, worrying the cap he held in two hands. "I have told you the truth, Major," he said.

"Yes," Gruber said. "Perhaps you have. You may leave."

The driver hurried out of the office.

"Send in the next one," Gruber said to a Gestapoman.

He sat back in his chair and lit a fresh cigar. He had questioned nine taxi drivers, and there were a dozen or more still waiting. He had asked his questions politely and reasonably because he considered himself a civilized man who did not resort to more hurtful methods until he was absolutely forced to do so. Perhaps that little story in the paper was not so far off after all. He was a very lucky man to have discovered it, he knew. He was fully aware of the effect it would have on his superiors. He could well imagine the reaction in Copenhagen. He did not even want to think about Berlin.

The driver who entered his office now was a smallish man with sparse gray hair, and he stood in front of Major Gruber with his hands shaking slightly. Major Gruber saw that he was frightened, and that was good. It always helped. It helped even more if he, Gruber, maintained calm and quiet because that approach was most effective with most Danes. These were a strong people, he thought, and violence only seemed to give them added strength.

"I am Major Gruber," he said affably and, he knew, totally unnecessarily.

The man shifted and said nothing.

"What is your name?" Gruber asked.

"Olesen, sir. Aksel Olesen."

Gruber drew on his cigar and made himself more comfortable. He very much enjoyed creating fear in others, but he assured himself it was only because it made his work easier.

"I am trying to find out something about two people who left the hospital in Elsinore two days ago. Do you follow me, Olesen?"

"Yes, sir."

"I have reason to believe they left together. I have also reason to believe they were not in any way ill, except for the illness of acting against the best interests of their country."

The man said nothing.

"I have further reason to believe they left the hospital by taxi. Does any of this sound familiar to you?" Gruber asked.

The man shuffled his feet and looked down at the floor. "Two people?"

"Two people. From the hospital. Two days ago."

Olesen thought for a moment. He remembered all right. Those bundles did seem odd even if the sister said they were filled with clothing. He could see a hard outline in the bundle the boy was carrying. He had tried not to think too much about it afterward because he was a small man in every way and he tried not to get mixed up in things that might be dangerous.

But he did not want to betray other Danes. Whatever they had done, it was plainly against the Germans, and while he was not in any way a fighter, he respected those who were.

"No," he said at last.

"You are certain?" Gruber asked easily.

"I don't remember any woman and boy," Olesen said.

Gruber broke the ash gently from his cigar and leaned forward. "I had not mentioned they were a woman and a boy," he said. "I just said 'two people.' "

He sat back and without raising his voice he said, "Now, you will surely have second thoughts—and you will tell me what I want to know."

Two minutes later the taxi driver was escorted from the room by a Gestapoman. He knew he had done something bad, but he had been unable to help it. It was not in his nature.

Now Gruber was galvanized into action. He picked up the telephone. "My car," he said. "And a second car with four men."

He looked with satisfaction at the information he had written down on his note pad. It all fit. And the address in Hellerup.

He stood up and took his heavy coat from the rack and put it on. The telephone rang. He picked up the receiver impatiently.

"Gruber," he said tersely. Then, "I cannot stop now. I am on my way out of the office on an important mission." Then, "Who?" Then, "Yes, of course."

He sat down slowly and put down his half-finished cigar. Then he said, "Yes, Herr Colonel." He straightened in astonishment. "Yes, I have seen the paper. It is quite a silly thing, isn't it? I'm sure there is some explanation, Herr Colonel. The Danish humor. My record here speaks for itself." He listened to the rasping voice that grated on the telephone like an iron file. "Yes, Herr Colonel, I will leave for Copenhagen immediately." He gripped the telephone. "Surely the Herr Colonel does not believe . . ."

But he realized by then that he was talking into a dead telephone.

29

PETER STOOD ALONE ON THE DOCK OF THE TUBORG BREWERY. The icy winter wind swept in from the Sound, burning his cheeks. He could see the lights of Sweden.

He had seen the lights every night for three nights. He and his mother had been taken from the lawyer's house to the brewery on schedule, but then things had gone wrong.

Returning from Sweden after an earlier transport, the little fishing boat in which they were to be taken to Sweden had been intercepted by a German patrol boat, and while the vessel was empty of human cargo, it also was empty of fish. The Danish captain had been taken to Copenhagen for questioning.

Another boat had been located but that developed engine trouble. They were still working on the engine.

Then the weather had turned bad. Violent winds churned the water, making passage impossible.

During those days Peter and Lise had been cared for by the Tuborg people, whose establishment was almost a small city in itself. Masses of people worked there, and most of them knew that cargo other than beer was being shipped from the company's docks. While they were very proud of their beer, they were even prouder of the other kind of shipment.

From those docks members of the Underground were whipped over to Sweden on secret missions against the enemy. To the docks from Sweden came men and women now trained in all the skills of destruction and death, and once deposited on Danish soil these men and women vanished into their country to use these skills. Other Underground workers wounded or injured too seriously or too obviously were sent to be treated in Swedish hospitals. From these docks hundreds of Danish Jews had been sent to safety, and from these docks messages went out in code, copies of Resistance papers, including that of Lars Andersen, sending out news of what was happening in the occupied country, news that was swiftly sent on to Britain and the world.

Now Peter stood there smelling the sea air, and he thought how it had been only a little more than a week since his mother and father and he had had dinner in the inn at Snekkersten.

"Peter."

He thought he heard his name, but it must have been the wind. He looked at the lights in the distance across the water. He wondered how it would be.

"Peter."

He turned and saw the big figure of Pastor Holm hurrying toward him. The priest was breathing hard, and Peter felt for the first time that his pastor was no longer a young man and that all of this, all the things he was doing these days, were things of young men. And yet he was doing them, as his father had done, as Sister Gerda had done.

"Peter, we have a boat," Holm said. "And the prediction is that the winds will die down a little. Come."

The burly priest and the slender, tall boy turned away from the water, and with the wind flailing their backs they hurried to another part of the dock area where a small fishing boat was bobbing in the savage water. Lise was waiting there, and Peter and his mother climbed aboard.

"One thing I must tell you before you go," Holm said, speaking loudly in the howl of the wind. "Our good German friend has been summoned to Copenhagen." The gleam appeared again in Pastor Holm's eyes. "For questioning." The priest stood back and wiped his eyes, watering from the wind. "God bless you both," he said. "And come back to Denmark."

The fishing captain pointed to an open hatch. Peter held his mother's hand as she got into the hold. Before he dropped down he looked again at the dock. The priest was wiping his eyes against the wind.

The hatch cover was slipped into place and they were in darkness. Then they felt the engine vibrating, and the boat began to move.

30

PETER STOOD BY HIS MOTHER'S SIDE ON THE PIER IN THE Swedish fishing village and looked back across the water. All they could see was water and then darkness.

"How long do you think we'll have to stay here?" Peter asked.

"I don't know," Lise said.

"Not long, I'll bet."

"Do you believe that?"

"Yes."

"Then perhaps you will be right. You have been right before."

They stared into the night. The wind was sad and lonely and cold.

"Peter," she said.

"Yes, Mother."

"You must never forget."

"Forget?"

"Everything. Everything that has happened. Your father most of all."

"I'll never forget him."

"You must remember that everything that has meaning for us is over there."

"Yes, Mother."

She jammed her hands in her coat pockets, and her eyes were wet, although the wind was blowing on her back.

"You'll grow up, Peter, and one day all of this will only be something you'll read in books. You'll even reach a time when you will get bored and lose interest and say, all right, there was a war and there were Nazis and they did terrible things, but that was years ago. Let's forget it and get on. And perhaps by then the Germans will be behaving decently, and it will seem practical to forget. But even then you must not forget."

"It's so dark," Peter said. "Across the water."

"Yes," she said. "But I believe you. I truly believe you. It will not be that way for long."

Lise took her hand out of her pocket and held it out to him, and gripping each other tightly they started toward the little Swedish village. Many of the cottages were already sprinkled with lights against the dark twilight of the winter morning.